THE CELLAR

Peter Beere

Copyright © 2025
All rights reserved

No part of this book may be reproduced by any means whatsoever without the prior approval and consent of the copyright holder.

The moral right of Peter Beere to be identified as the author of this work has been asserted by him in accordance with Section 77 of the Copyright, Designs and Patents Act 1988

This book is an adaptation of the novel
AT GEHENNA'S DOOR
published by Scholastic Publications in 1997
and authored by Peter Beere

NECROPHOBE

A being which is consistently successful at avoiding its own death or is apparently shunned by death itself.

(From Greek: *nekros*, corpse + *phobos,* fearing.)

Professor Jonathan Mort-Coves.

From:
The Science of Necrophobes:
A propositional work.

1

The four girls had lost their way somewhere amongst the rocks and trees – which caused them no surprise. Their phones had ceased receiving a signal a while back – they were in a proverbial 'dead zone'. And the path was so overgrown and canopied by boughs that to advance along its route at all was quite an admirable feat: to have to stop and check a paper map in brambles shoulder-deep would have been one act too many.

The girls' endeavours were also hampered by a savage-hearted storm which stained the winter sky with a premature twilight. The cold wind in the trees and the rain which hissed like angry snakes hampered rational thought.

Jade pointed up a slope towards what looked like a cave, and said, 'We should shelter there.'

Her three friends followed her, scrambling up a steep slick bank which tried to flip them off each time they advanced, so it seemed that not just the storm, but the very land itself set out to thwart their progress. They had prepared quite well for their trip – packed items and necessities to cope with wind and rain – but nobody on earth could have foreseen what the world had opted to throw at them that day. It was as if the gods of storms had decided to strap on their swords and wage celestial warfare.

Just to complete their luck the cave turned out to be a deception after all. It was nothing but a shallow alcove – a depression in the rock which continued above until it formed a minor cliff. It was filled with dead roots and trailing ferns, with the smell of mouldering earth, and the stink from rotting leaves.

There was nothing to be done but huddle in a bunch, and gaze forlornly out at the strengthening storm. They watched forked lightning flash over distant hills. Listened to thudding rain and the wind's moans in the trees. They heard a nearby bough go crashing to earth, its strength and spirit sapped.

'We can't wait here,' Amy said, tugging at her heavy brown curls. 'It will be getting dark soon. We need some place to stay.'

Her older sister, Louisa, agreed with her. 'We need to reach that next site. An Airbnb would do; even a hotel at a push. We could phone home for some cash. They could pay by card – '

The eldest of the four gave a snort. The athletically built Caroline was not impressed by that. 'There are no sites around here,' she said. 'The nearest one is ten kilometres south – we'd not get there for hours. I said at the last crossroads that we had to start heading south, but no, you had to lead us here.'

Amy said that she thought this was south. Caroline gave another snort. 'South, as opposed to what?'

'South like the way we should go! I used that new compass that my dad gave me. Which was working fine until Louisa went and trod on it and now it's like a map of the stars.'

'I didn't tread on it – you dropped it right in front of me!'

'And you checked the coordinates on your phone. So don't try blaming it on me.'

That caused a certain huffiness: and a minute or so of silence ensued.

It was Jade who broke the silence. 'So how long do we plan on hanging around here?' she said, after she'd studied their sodden paper map. 'Because we're not on here. Not unless this entire map's wrong.'

'Oh great, that's all we need – we're not even on the map now!' Louisa slumped to her knees. 'We're stuck in this backside of a cave with half a pack of Dairylea Dunkers and an assortment of soaking clothes. And we all know whose fault it is.'

'I've already told you, don't blame it on me, Lou! You had a look at the compass too.' Amy looked out at the rainswept trees, the blackness, the roiling sky. 'I didn't want to come in the first place.'

'Despite all that, we can't stay here,' Caroline said, steeling herself, 'unless we want to starve. We'll have to head somewhere.'

She looked around vaguely, in search of clues. 'I'm open to ideas of the practical sort.'

The rather sombre Jade said, 'We could say a prayer to the kind spirits of the earth.'

'Brilliant, Jade. Thanks a lot.'

The girls set off down the slope: when lost, the instinctive thing to do is to proceed downhill.

They knew that they were a considerable distance away from the nearest main road. Some distance further still from the comfort of a town. To find even an isolated cottage or farmhouse would have been a lucky break – they had not passed one in hours.

They had to come up with something, though – they needed at the very least a track. Even a spot like this must possess lanes and paths. Surely nowhere in Britain was *that* remote, was it?

The girls quickly found out.

The afternoon became more murky still – the rain's veils ever more intense – and the wind gathered itself into one long bleak howl. Battered bruised and exhausted the four scaled another bank to discover, to their vast relief, that they had chanced upon a path. Not one of the best tracks in the world – merely a line of cinders, dirt and logs – but a solid route nonetheless.

One arm set off eastward, through a landscape of dead grey furze. The other headed north, through a terrain of skeletal trees.

Caroline flipped her lucky 50-pence coin. If it was 'heads' they would plough eastwards...

The coin sent the four girls north.

Amy said, 'It will be just our luck when we find somewhere if everyone's gone away. They've probably gone off for the holidays – which is what we should have done. Next time we get a break I'm heading for the sun.'

Louisa said, 'If you don't cheer up you'll be doing it on your own, because we shan't come along.'

'You *have* to come, Lou. You're my sister, that's the rule. It's a golden rule.'

'And who says that?' said Louisa.

'I do,' Amy said dismally. 'You dragged me along on this trip –'

'Amy, you begged to come!'

'It sounded like fun back then…'

Still the storm intensified, and still moody pools of darkness dripped like poison from the sky. The girls passed through dense groves of creaking, wind-tossed trees. They put black birds to flight – huge things with flaring wings like furious avatars stripped from the walls of mines. The birds wheeled against the clouds, framed by a searing burst of magnesium-bright lightning. The enormous flock then streamed away south as if it was a fragment of the cloak of Death itself. Cackling, cawing – as wild as the enraged sky. For a long time after the flock had disappeared harsh cries came drifting back to the girls, like mocking taunts flaunting on the wind.

'We have to find somewhere soon,' said Jade, reluctantly switching on her weakening flashlight. Its narrow beam probed ahead but the muddy track in front of them vanished into a sudden dip, and everything beyond that was hidden. It was as though a great secret was crouching out of sight, secure from prying eyes.

The girls thought that there must be a house or farm somewhere nearby, for they could smell wood smoke on the air. They could detect the scent of roasting meat, and the sickly tang of basting fat. They hoped – oh, how they hoped – that they had reached some help at last. They badly needed sanctuary…

2

A trail of brilliant light blazed across the purple sky, and the four girls froze as one. Just for an instant, though it remained imprinted on their brains, they glimpsed the refuge they had sought as it reared out of the gloom. Not a quaint moorland inn, not a warm B&B; what they had seen was quite macabre. More bleak and gloomy than any haunted house. More lonely than a ship lost on uncharted seas. With massive buttresses, imposing shutters, iron railings and towers apparently designed by an insane architect, the place ahead looked more like a mausoleum than a home.

'It's not ideal,' Caroline said. 'Although I suppose it could be worse.'

'Exactly how?' Louisa said glumly. 'Do you mean that at least there are no corpses hanging from the walls? No blood-drenched Rottweilers prowling beyond the gates?'

'At least it has a fire. Check out the chimney smoke.'

'Check out my sinking heart.'

As the girls approached the wrought-iron gates which guarded the eerie house, they saw multiple signs of deep decay.

The old lock had rusted; ancient hinges had snapped. Slabs had slipped from the outer wall, thrust out by brooding shrubs. There was a pungent smell of gas – the kind of acrid stench which seeps from sewers and swamps. Somewhere beyond the house there must have been a tract of marsh; it was fortunate, perhaps, that they'd not roamed from the track. They might have found their end – sinking through layers of mud – watched by that roiling sky.

'There's a nameplate on the gate.' Jade pointed with her torch. 'What does that say – *Gethsemane*?'

'No – it's *Gehenna*,' Louisa said, leaning closer, sweeping her heavy fringe out of her dark brown eyes. 'A strange name for a house. I think it's from the bible. It means something like 'place of torment'.'

They advanced across the mud-swamped yard, almost rendered senseless by thick waves of the foul gas.

They approached the main door: solid, heavy and closed.

Amy said, 'Ring the bell.'

Caroline said, 'There is no bell. There's an old brass knocker.'

'Try that.'

'Are you sure that's wise? I'm not keen on this place.'

But Amy was impetuous, reckless and tired of storms. She said, 'Are you afraid?'

'Oh no – I love this stuff! I get up in the mornings to embrace it.'

Caroline took a long deep breath, reached out one cautious hand, grasped the heavy knocker…

Prongs of lightning pierced the clouds as the girls awaited a response to Caroline's hesitant knock. No hint of movement was apparent in the house. No glimmer of light showed – no shutters were flung back. The place loomed like a tomb – ominously still and quiet.

The door remained stubbornly shut.

After a time the girls moved on with the hope that they might locate a less forbidding entrance. They followed a muddy pathway which skirted the left side of the house, past lean-tos, barns and sheds, and what looked like a large refuse pit. They gave that particular spot a considerable berth. The last thing they needed was to stumble into it.

There was a dreadful odour rising from the maw of the pit. The gamy reek of household waste, mingled with rotting meat. It was probably all meant to have been burnt to ash but the inclement weather might have set that task back.

The girls' attention was diverted from the nauseating stench by the appearance from the gloom of a weathered porch, with a black oak door beyond.

Someone was singing in a room behind the door. The notes mixed with a noise of kitchen pots and pans. Someone was sharpening a knife with slow, deliberate strokes – using a grinding stone. So like the shriek of a dental drill was the sound of steel on stone that it made the girls hold back, made them wait in the rain. They flinched as thunder crashed and lightning rent the sky directly overhead.

Eventually Caroline summoned up enough nerve to step inside the porch, and give a timid knock. Nobody answered, although the grinding stopped. In fact, everything stopped, as if life itself held its breath. The pots and pans fell quiet, the strident singing ceased. Even the storm decreased. Caroline tapped more loudly but still nobody came. She gripped the door handle, and it turned with a solid click. She eased the door open, and the stench of roasting meat spilled out on a pungent tide.

The room beyond was not the most welcoming place that Caroline had ever seen. It was a grimy kitchen – massive, but mainly empty. Just a bare square table, an old range and a sink. A brace of dead pheasants was hanging from a hook to one side of the door. And a heap of wrinkled vegetables had been carelessly crammed into one corner of the room: potatoes, carrots, beets. They had been grown in Gehenna's fields – but clearly had not thrived in the peaty moorland soil.

'Go in – ' Amy whispered.

'You've not seen inside yet. I'm not sure we should.'

Caroline was almost rigid with tension but found herself pressed in by the three girls at her back, who were anxious to find some warmth. Their minds were more concerned with a sudden increase in the rain and a strengthening of the wind. In fact, so eager were they that they shoved past Caroline and only thought to check when they had bundled through the doorway. At which point they all paused – the way that a group of rabbits might pause when suddenly faced by a fox.

'Say something ... ' Amy hissed, as all eyes settled on the only person in the room – a woman of startling grotesqueness. The woman was enormous, carrying levels of fat almost beyond human scale. Ancient and maggot-white, with thinning grey hair tied loosely back. Dressed in a long white gown. Showing bare, massive feet. Stirring a simmering stew-pan.

'Tell her we're harmless ... '

Caroline cleared her throat. The woman gave a start and almost dislodged the pan. Her stirring-spoon slipped out of her fat-fingered grip and clattered on the floor.

'I'm sorry we startled you. We knocked ... ' Louisa said. 'We knocked – but no one came.'

Jade said, 'We've been on a camping trip but got lost on the moors.' The old woman might well have been deaf, for all the response she gave. She simply bent down to grab the fallen spoon, wiped it across her sleeve, and carried on stirring.

'My sister is unused to welcoming strangers,' hissed a new voice in the room. An old man had been watching them, unnoticed all this time. Crouched in an inglenook, concealed by veils of gloom. He now rose to his feet. He was withered, gaunt and pale, but strong in hand and eye.

'Don't be alarmed,' he said. (The girls looked fit to scream.) 'There is only we two here – no more surprises in store. Come in, take off your coats. Relax, try to get warm.'

The sibilant old man stepped from his gloomy nook as though leaving a cave. He helped the girls to shrug off their packs, saw them sat down. He found a stool for himself, set it down in their midst. So close was he that they could smell his clothes, which reeked of mould and earth. He was not cordial; nor was he unfriendly. He seemed, if anything, inquisitive and alert. It was almost as though he thought the girls might have brought something of use or worth.

'So, it was not through choice that you approached our door?' he said.

'Not really,' Caroline said. 'We set off this morning, walking from Torristown. We planned to reach Blacktor, use the campsite there.'

The old man's ears pricked up. 'The campsite at Blacktor – you'll never get there now. Oh no, you've missed it – that's not this way at all. There is very little to be found in these parts; some farms, this house, the moors. It's a desolate region.'

'We noticed that all right,' Amy said, with a sigh …

3

Although the kitchen was large, it soon became cluttered with the four girls and their packs in it. There was barely sufficient space left for the old woman to cook. After a few moments, frustration made her tense. Her brother came to her aid, murmured some soothing words, then beckoned the girls away.

He led them though an empty hallway, showed them into another room which, once a comfortable lounge, had long since been conquered by dust. He threw back grey covers to reveal antique chairs beneath. He roughly brushed them down with his hand and said, 'Sit here.'

The man tossed some spindly twigs into an empty hearth. He added larger logs, some paper and a flame. He watched grey smoke rise up – reluctantly at first. Then stronger. The logs blazed.

'One certainly needs a fire on a night as bad as this,' he said, his gaze flicking to the gloomy room's huge windows.

The girls stared with him, to confirm that it was night. No one could disagree; there could not be more night. The scene beyond the house was one of unremitting black, save for odd lightning bursts.

'As black as a coal face,' he went on, crossing the room. He tugged a braided cord and curtains slid across the panes. He laughed. 'Now we are all alone in this nice haven of warmth. Safe from a hostile world.'

'We mustn't stay for too long,' Jade said uncomfortably, glancing around as if she sought support from her silent friends. 'We're not planning to stay. We just need some directions … '

'Oh no, it's far too late. You'll never reach Blacktor now; it's far better you stay here. We have entertained before; you are not the first hikers to become lost on the moors.'

'But it's … '

'No trouble.'

The old man gave a thin, cold smile. In fact, so thin was it that they could almost see right through. Almost into his thoughts, where nothing smiled at all – as if his brain was stone.

After a few minutes the old man left the room to attend to his huge sister who, he had explained, became nervous on her own. The four girls sat mutely in his absence, scared to move: each too timid to say, 'This place is weird'. They merely looked around, hearts sinking at the dust, the silence and the gloom.

The place was so quiet with the heavy curtains drawn that they felt wholly removed from the familiar comforts of their world. Even the storm's fury strained to penetrate far through the building's massive walls.

'Those two are pretty freaky,' Amy said, becoming the first to shatter the tense silence. 'They are bad fruitcakes on overload.'

'Hush,' murmured Caroline. 'They live out in the wilds, kilometres away from anywhere. They're not used to visitors – that's probably all it is. At least they took us in.'

'It probably threw them, us four simply turning up.' This came from Louisa, who was closest to the fire. She was staring into its depths as if, within the flames, secrets might be unearthed. 'So let's stay calm, and not get overwrought.'

'Oh yes let's!' Amy paced the floor, too restless to remain sitting down. 'Stay calm in the 'House of Gloom' – with that pair of ghouls waiting to appear in the next 'Scream' movie!'

All conversation ceased as the girls picked up the sound of someone in the hall. The door swung open, and the old man stepped inside. His eyes seemed strangely bright, as if fed by an inner fire. He said, 'Martha says you must join in our meal; she is cooking extra food.'

'That's very kind of you.' Caroline eyed her nervous friends. It was now falling to her to be their spokesperson. She said, 'And after that we should continue on our way; we'll feel much better then. We don't want to be a nuisance … '

'You're no trouble at all. In fact, it's rather nice to have outsiders here. Helps us to keep abreast and stops us from stagnating. Or becoming quite insane!'

The girls followed their peculiar host into a gloomy room large enough to entertain a feast. A dust-covered table was laid out with six places. Ample space still remained to seat some dozen more. The room around was bare, though nonetheless quite warm; a huge fire saw to that.

The man bade them sit down, then cried, 'Bring on the feast!'
The grotesque Martha lurched in, lugging a steaming pan.
She plonked it down.
The girls gazed unhappily at the gruel-like stew within …

4

By the time the so-called meal ended, the four girls realized that it was far too late to leave. Outside the wicked storm still rampaged and the rain was like hammers on the window panes. Lightning inflamed the sky with its pyrotechnic rage. A wild wind lashed the trees which loomed behind the house, making them groan like wounded beasts.

None but an imbecile or a truly desperate soul would plan to journey far through a tempest such as that. The girls felt desperate, but they were not imbeciles: they knew well enough that they were stuck.

So, somewhat reluctantly, they accepted the couple's offer of accommodation for the night. Not in the creepy house, though; they weren't too keen on that. They doubted they'd sleep well in such strange company, though they did not say as much. They were not quite so blunt. They simply said, 'We've imposed enough.'

Instead, they took the option of sleeping in a barn: bedding themselves down in straw, with their sleeping bags pulled up tight.

The old man said, 'If you're sure?'

'We're sure – the barn sounds fine.'

'As you wish,' he said, shrugging.

They trailed their mysterious host to a rickety wooden barn and helped him heave open the doors. They waited while he lit an ancient oil lantern which he hung from a rusting hook. Its dancing yellow light failed to reach all the walls. But it was strong enough to reveal a small square byre, packed with dusty grey straw.

'Will that be suitable?'

'It's fine,' Caroline said.

'You will find an earth closet at the far side of the yard.'

'A what?'

'An outside latrine.'

'Oh.'

'With a water pump so that you can get washed. And if you hear anything – it will probably just be rats.' The old man glanced around, with a slightly wary frown. 'Or possibly a fox. We do get them around here.'

With that he shuffled out.

'That was something of a worrying frown,' Amy said uneasily, as soon as the old man left. 'There's no one else in here, is there?'

'He would have said something, I'm sure,' Caroline said. 'Relax, we'll be all right.'

'Oh sure. Have you checked that roof? It could come crashing down on us at any minute.'

'Well it's a choice Amy - bedding down in here or sleeping in a room along a hall from that old man. Do you want to sleep near him?'

'I don't want to sleep near anyone tonight. The weather's not even supposed to be like this at this time of year.'

'It's climate change,' said Jade. 'We have offended the gods of the earth.'

'Excellent, Jade. That's just what we need. I'm sure on that note we'll have a great night.'

5

In spite of the frenzied, howling wind and the relentless battering of the rain the girls – exhausted – slept reasonably well. Their weary eyes adjusted to the lightning and their nerves ceased to leap as thunder crashed in salvos right outside. Any rats in the barn kept a discreet distance; no prowling foxes barked. In fact, the major cause of disturbance was the proximity of the eerie house, and the tension it evoked. Its aura was so bleak that a hibernating bear would have had to keep waking up to check …

* * *

'Wake up – it's after ten.'

Caroline jerked awake. 'So late? Where did that go? What's the weather like outside?'

'Wet, wild and windy,' said a glum and sombre Jade. 'Still pouring with rain. No break in the clouds. And the wind has started gusting like a hurricane. I don't think we're going to be going anywhere soon. You can hardly see the path, it's almost washed away.'

Caroline's head slumped back on the straw.

'Are the others up yet?'

'Amy's still fast asleep. Lou's gone to the house to see what's going on. Get a weather forecast.'

'She'll be lucky,' Caroline said. 'They're still living in the Stone Age here. They're probably waiting for a carrier pigeon to arrive.'

* * *

It was not the best of fun braving that angry storm, pummelled by vicious rain.

Lou's feet struggled for purchase on the slick mud of the yard. She bent herself practically double in her attempts to combat the wind. It snatched at her waterproofs and nearly made her retreat in defeat to the barn. At times it seemed almost to be singing: *'Don't go towards the house. Do not step inside those doors – do not tread Gehenna's halls – '* But of course that was just the wind. None but the fanciful would credit wind with thought.

'Hello,' Lou called, as she stepped cautiously past the door which led from the porch.

Gehenna appeared deserted; the dim kitchen was still. A passageway beyond was empty, bleak and chill. Not the faintest of sounds came from the master of the house, nor his corpulent sister.

Maybe there was just the slightest whisper in a far-off lonely hall, but that might only have been the wind curiously drifting from room to room.

Slowly the door creaked shut behind her, helped along by the spurt of a breeze. The two dead pheasants swayed on their hooks. Their dead eyes staring nowhere.

Lou walked cautiously on. Along the hallway, past the stairs. Two closed doors stood ahead.

'Is anyone there?'

Her own voice echoed back to her. It was the only sound, it seemed, in the entire house. She ventured a few more steps and pushed open the first door. Saw the remains of last night's meal.

After several more strides she reached the second door. She tapped on it. There was no reply. She grasped the handle, pushed the door back and peered within. A huge four-poster bed loomed at her through the greyness of the morning light. Was there somebody sprawled on it, or not? She wasn't sure: veiled curtains obscured her view.

She would have to step inside and pull back the hanging drapes. She would have to take the risk someone might get a fright. If they would only speak. If they would only move –

'Please don't enter that room!'

Lou's head snapped around. She saw the strange old man at the midpoint of the stairs. She had not heard him coming – he must have moved like thistledown over silk. He clutched an armful of logs on his way to build a fire. His eyes were cold and pale, like those of dead fish on a slab. 'That is my sister's room. She can't climb the steep stairs so has to sleep down here.'

'I'm sorry,' Lou said. 'I called, but no one heard.'

'No matter – I am here now, ready to soothe all woes. How may I help you, my child?'

6

'Lou's been gone for a while,' Jade said, checking her phone with its rapidly fading battery. 'You ought to go and find her … '

Amy let out a groan. 'I've barely woken up. You go; she can't be far.'

'Lou isn't my sister. She might have wound up lost.'

'I might get lost *myself.*' Amy snuggled down again in her thick sleeping bag, pulled it over her head, mumbled out of its depths, 'I'll go in five minutes. She could be back by then.'

'I'll tell her how much you cared.'

* * *

'The outlook?' said the man. 'One hardly needs a weather forecast for that, you have tested it yourself in the yard. As for your offer of help for your keep, that is very kind. But I assure you, child, everything is in hand. You and your companions should try to relax. Try to enjoy your brief respite as Gehenna's guests.'

'We shall,' Lou murmured, straining to produce a smile. 'Let's hope it's not for too long!' She gave a nervous laugh.

The old man's face revealed the thinnest of half-smiles.

'It will just take as long as it takes,' he said.

* * *

Lou rejoined the others in the barn where they talked and sighed and muttered with frustration at the persistence of the storm.

Despite the wild weather they weren't glad to be inside, nor did they feel inclined to extend their sojourn any longer than necessary. The place was simply too creepy. They weighed up all their limited options. Reached the decision that they would leave. It was the only decision to take.

Out of common politeness they would have to walk across to Gehenna to thank their sibling hosts. Thank them for last night's food. *Bleagh!* And their comfortable beds. *Ha!* And the unparalleled company.

'Did you get the old man's name?' asked Jade, as they fought their way through the wind towards the monstrous house.

'He said it's Franklin,' said Lou, battling to keep her hood fastened as stinging rain pounded her face. 'The family name is Jilkes. He said that some people call this house 'the old Jilkes place'.'

'Is that a famous name?'

'I don't know,' Lou said. 'But he rather seemed to hope that I would be impressed.'

'Well I hope you were.'

'Oh I was. I nearly fell over backwards in my astonishment.'

The four reached Gehenna's porch and felt themselves shrinking back from the building's atmosphere. The place seemed to breathe gloominess in the same way that a flame breathes light. It seemed to spread outside, enfold them, grip like ice. Its presence was so strong that it was almost like a wall: hard and resilient.

For several moments the girls froze on the spot. They felt as though a hand had reached down through their throats. Its fingers clutched their hearts, their lungs, controlled their limbs. They had to fight to draw in breath.

But at last Lou knocked and, as before, was met by silence from within. She pushed the door back and led her three friends inside. They all huddled like sheep, a few paces to the rear.

'Where are they?' muttered Jade.

'Must be further inside.'

'Lead on bold one; we're right behind. One for all and – you go on.'

The dim hallway was still. Martha's bedroom was locked. The dining room looked bare.

The girls waited, listening to Gehenna's eerie sounds: the draughts which prowled the stairs, the creaking of old doors. Nothing human emerged, no voices or footsteps.

'Maybe they've gone out,' said Jade.

But even as Jade spoke a stooped figure appeared from a doorway the girls had overlooked. It was the disconcerting Franklin, emerging from a space tucked underneath the stairs – an alcove deep within the shade.

The old man was carrying a long-handled spade, and had thick brown dirt clinging to his hands. A caking of mud was plastered over his knees.

He was startled to discover the girls standing in the hall, but quickly recovered himself and offered them his austere grey smile.

He said, 'I have been downstairs ensuring that our cellar is secure. It has been known to flood in the past.'

It fell to Caroline to break the awkward hush which followed Franklin's words. She said, 'We just called to say thank you for putting us up last night. We think we'll set off soon, make our way to Blacktor.'

The old man gave a laugh: a dry and brittle thing, like the snapping of spindly twigs.

'It is impossible to leave now,' he said, 'and there is nowhere that you could go. When the rain pours down like this, all the moor lanes block with mud. Flash floods, uprooted trees, landslides and hidden bogs: you would not achieve a hundred yards. No, you must stay here so we know that you're all safe.'

'That's very kind of you, but – '

'It is not mere kindness which offers you this advice. I am sure you would do the same for other people in your plight.'

Caroline tried to smile. She really tried her best.

But nothing much emerged.

'Well done,' Amy muttered when Franklin left the hallway. 'Now you've got us really stuck!'

'Well what was I supposed to do?' Caroline said indignantly. 'You heard what he said – we'd get trapped on the moors.'

'At least we could have *looked*, checked the route out for ourselves.'

'Well you go out and take a look, Amy – that is totally fine by me. Then come back and give us your report, tell us we'll all be perfectly safe. And try not to sink into a bog while you're doing it.'

'You gave in much too soon. He bullied you into staying.'

'Well okay then, I gave in! Next time you can do all the talking. We'll see how much better you get on … '

7

Regardless of the pros and cons of remaining at the house, the decision had been made. In fact, it soon became a matter without any choice: the storm's wrath grew apace and its wilfulness knew no bounds. Tridents of lightning plunged through steel-grey clouds; thunderclaps shook the earth. None but the reckless would venture on the moor in a tempest like that – best to wait and endure. Let the demented gods of heaven wage their wars. Let them expend their rage.

Having disposed of his logs, Franklin returned to the girls and said, 'You must treat this house as your own. I have to warn you, though, that Gehenna is very old and – although structurally sound – many of her features have decayed over time. The attic in particular is one area to avoid, and you must exercise great care below.'

'I think it's unlikely that we'll be going into the cellar,' said Jade.

'But it is worth a look. The extent of its reach is a thing to behold. It has so many rooms and tunnels that it may better be described as 'Gehenna's Labyrinth'. It can be quite an unnerving place, but you should not be too alarmed, any noises you hear will most probably be the wind. For those of you who might be keen on the past, there are some things down there of, well, great 'significance'.'

Nobody was overly keen on taking a trip downstairs, despite the old man's 'helpful' words. Nor were the girls particularly elated by the arrangements for the lunch they had offered to make as recompense for their keep. It was not the work involved so much as the disgusting state that the kitchen was in. As far as the four could tell it had probably not been cleaned since the invention of the lightbulb.

The amount of grime and decay within the room had virtually become an art form.

The floor was swimming and the walls were smeared with grease. The pans heaped in the sink looked as though they had lain since the last Ice Age. Every last plate was cracked. Every last cup was chipped. Even a starving dog would have retched at what that kitchen had to offer.

'Maybe we could clean up?' Jade offered tentatively. 'Before we start to cook.'

The old man grunted. 'Do you find the room dirty?'

'It's just ... there are no clean plates.'

'Use the ones from last night.'

'They're still covered with grease.'

'There is not much wrong with grease – one could keep grease for years, and add to it each year. However, if it helps to make you happy... ' Franklin gave a careless shrug. 'You may do as you wish; this place is now your home. You will need to boil water in the pans. Fetch fresh water from the well. We have no water piped in.'

8

Caroline and Louisa volunteered to fill the pans using a large bucket that had been used for steeping clothes. They were given directions to a borehole in the yard, which sounded reasonable fun until they left the house. At which point the storm reminded them that novelties can soon wear off. Wave after wave of blinding rain came on a bitter wind. A wind Arctic-cold and as brutal as a wall. It forced them off their feet, slapped them into the mud, and sent their pail bouncing away.

'Oh no! Quick – grab it!' Lou cried above the wind. She made a desperate lunge, half-grasped it, then felt it slip. She scrambled to her feet – got captured by the wind – then lost all control.

She was flung headlong across the open yard. She stumbled through the mud and almost plunged into the refuse pit.

She saw piles of rotting food. Discarded meat turning into slime.

Then the wind drove her past.

* * *

Back in the cold kitchen Franklin was doing his best to act like a normal host. It wasn't easy for him; he clearly had no great experience of low-level chitchat. He struggled to find words: indeed, he strained to find even a friendly expression. It seemed his main look was a sly gaze: a furtive, hungry stare best suited to a fox. He was not helped at all by the fact that his narrow eyes were glittering and icy. He would struggle in any situation.

'So then,' he said at last, 'you have been walking on the moors? Exploring, camping and sightseeing. Enjoying your youthful enthusiasm.'

Jade said, 'It was mostly just camping. There isn't that much sightseeing to see.'

'That is true,' he said. 'The moors can be fairly bleak.'

'You're telling me. I guess it's the wrong time of year; we should have come in spring instead of autumn.'

'Hmm. Possibly so. Why *did* you come now – if you don't mind me asking?'

Jade shrugged. 'It was one of those things. We met up at a summer camp, got on well and planned some things. The first chance we got we thought, 'We'll set off now'. I guess we were hasty and should have checked the maps more. You can act a bit too fast, it seems.'

'I don't think it's that,' said the old man. 'You were simply unfortunate that the weather changed.'

'I guess,' said Jade. 'Although it doesn't really feel that way.'

'But look at the positives. At least you are safe now. Now that you have come to us.'

'I guess,' said Jade.

'Comfortable and warm. Absolutely secure … '

Jade flinched beneath his twisted gaze.

* * *

Caroline and Louisa strove to return across the yard with the brimming pail still intact.

The storm seemed demented. The wind was ballooning their coats - it turned them into sails and almost lifted the girls aloft. Their feet scarcely touched the earth so massive was the pressure of air against them.

And they quickly began floundering, labouring to stay upright on the treacherous, slimy ground – struggling to make any headway at all against the remorseless and strength-sapping wind. The rain had fashioned itself into eye-blasting sheets which rendered them almost blind.

They lost their grip on the pail, which spilled its contents and went bouncing away – and with it all attempts to hold on to their course. The pair had no choice but to give in to the wind and run wherever it had a mind.

Caroline let out a shriek as she was forced perilously close to a pile of sharpened jutting logs. A roll of barbed wire loomed towards her, then veered itself away. Rusting machinery lurched forwards, bundled fence posts, abandoned tyres. She tried to steer her way around an overgrown bed of shrubs but hit a low wall, and got herself confused.

She skinned her ankle, then tumbled sideways. She cracked her head on something then saw a parade of stars – a wall of mud, a lot of metal, and streaks of her own blood. She clambered to her feet – still half-stunned, still bemused. Tried to look around …

'Are you there, Lou?'

She could hear Lou calling, faintly, but where was she? Where was the ancient house: the kitchen and sanctuary? She lurched blindly ahead, not noticing the yawning pit …

'Lou? Are you this way?'

Though she wasn't having a truly great time herself, Lou was nonetheless better placed than Caroline to survive the wind. She had reached the shelter of the house, but turned around just in time to see Caroline's battle end with startling abruptness. One moment she was there, albeit unsteady; the next, she'd disappeared.

She had fallen headfirst into the refuse pit. It might have almost have been funny, except Lou didn't think it was. That pit was ominously deep and Caroline didn't reappear. It was as if she had been devoured.

Lou cried, 'Are you all right, Caroline?' but the wind swallowed her words. Someone standing right alongside her would have been hard-pressed to hear. So she waited and she watched, and she kept her fingers crossed, but Caroline did not appear from the stinking pit.

Lou ran as best she could through the hampering wind, and crouched down beside the pit. Great peals of thunder crashed directly overhead. Lightning bolts plunged to earth and the air crackled with static. The whole sky seemed ablaze; the darkened earth leapt and quaked while the walls of the nearby house shook. Its upper reaches wailed like terrified beasts. The wind tugged at weathered boards and shutters, slammed on doors. Tiles skittered off the roof and landed in pools of mud with *splats* like dropped, ripe fruit. And everything appeared on the brink of destruction.

'Hey - Caroline! Are you OK in there?'

Caroline squinted up at Lou. 'Oh yes. I'm totally owning things down here.'

She was lying winded and helpless on a bed of slithering refuse, the stench of which passed the reek to high heaven. Every time she tried to move she merely caused herself to flounder further in. Which would have been quite bad enough on its own, but Caroline found herself facing matters even worse. All kinds of junk and waste had been tossed into the pit. Amongst the worst of all was the object resting by her face. The half-eaten skull of a dead sheep.

Even that skull proved to have worse things to reveal: things which came wriggling from the sockets of its eyes. Things that were cadaver-white and newborn puppy-blind. Bloated, slimy maggots.

Caroline shrieked. 'Lou! Get me out of here! There are maggots crawling round my face!'

'Right. I'll go and fetch help – '

'Don't leave me alone!' Caroline shrieked again. Her nerves wanted to snap. 'I can't stand things like this, Lou! I can't do anything that squirms around.'

'I can't get to you, Caroline – I'll fall in myself.'

'Lou – I'm not fooling around down here. You have to get me out!'

'The maggots won't harm you. They only eat dead flesh.'

'That isn't a consolation!'

9

It was clear that Caroline could not climb from the pit, and was in truly desperate straits. The more she struggled the more helpless she became, and the further her legs sank into the morass. Unless she remained completely still it was quite feasible that she would disappear for good.

Nor could Lou reach her; her flailing fingertips fell centimetres short of her friend's outstretched hand.

Several times Lou herself appeared on the brink of sliding in as well.

'It's hopeless, Caroline! I really do need help.'

'Well make it quick!'

'I'll be two minutes, I promise, nothing more. Try to stop thrashing around, you're making matters worse.'

'Well aren't I the fool, then? You ought to come down here – see how you get on with the thrashing around thing!'

'Just try to keep calm – '

'Oh sure – I'll sing a song. What a pity I didn't bring a book with me.'

'I'll be as quick as I can.'

'Don't hurry back on my account. They're only maggots, Lou!'

When Lou got back to the house there was nobody in sight, nor did she hear a sound.

She started shouting, but no one answered her. She ran from room to room. But every room stood bare. She thundered up the stairs, taking an advanced course in what is known as 'Murphy's Law'.

'Murphy's Law' simply states that if something can go wrong, then nine times out of ten it will. That light at the end of the tunnel you were hoping for, will almost certainly be from an onrushing train.

* * *

Amy and Jade, grown bored, had ventured off to explore some more of the old house. After a brief search they'd unearthed further rooms; the hallway did not end just past Martha's bedroom. Another hall appeared, so cunningly designed it seemed like a mere slat of gloom. It did make sense, though; the ground floor had to be considerably larger than what had been seen so far. In truth, they had not seen too much, but both sensed that – if they stayed – they would encounter a great deal more.

They wandered through the doorway of a dim, dusty room – once a fine library. Largely abandoned now, its shelves had been stripped clean. They jutted from the walls like the ribs of hungry beasts. In the centre of the room was a table, so dusty it seemed to be wrapped in a shroud.

They passed a second door in the room, but it was locked and had no key. The library's grimy windows looked out across the yard. The girls wiped dust from the panes and gazed out, but could not see much: grey rain, a tract of mud. No sign of Caroline or Lou from that angle. If they rose up on tiptoe they could just make out two barns. And Gehenna's outer wall – capped by a line of spikes. And trees like skeletons.

A rustle of clothing warned of Franklin's approach, which was more than his feet did. They propelled him silently across the library floor. He seemed almost to glide – surprising for his age. He wore a sly half-grin as if he knew something it was better not to know. But by the time he reached the girls his strange grin had disappeared. It had gone so completely they weren't even sure it had been there. When he stood at Amy's side the only look he showed was one of deep concern.

'So dreadful,' he muttered, as he gazed out at the storm. 'Not helping you at all. Such fearsome thunder – '

As he spoke the sky gods roared.

'Lightning beyond belief – '

Tridents of lightning flashed.

'Noises to wake the dead – '

Somewhere a door was slammed – shutters banged – roof tiles clattered crashed and smashed.

'No hope of leaving us for some time yet, I fear.'

Jade said, 'It looks that way. Looks as though we have been trapped.'

'How true,' Franklin said sadly. But for the briefest span his sly grin reappeared.

Straight after Franklin had spoken, a tense and breathless Lou burst into the library.

She said, 'It's Caroline! She accidentally fell into that awful pit where you dump all your waste.'

'Oh dear,' Franklin murmured. 'What a disgusting thing to happen to someone. And on your first morning! How on earth will you cope if you're compelled to stay here for any length of time.'

'What?' Lou was quite nonplussed by what appeared to be levity on Franklin's part. She said, 'She's helpless! She can't climb up the sides!'

'How very appalling. They are so steep and slippery and wet.'

'Will you help to get her out?' He made Lou feel totally foolish and naïve.

'A frail old man like me?'

But the old man's teasing quickly passed and he went outside to help, moving with surprising speed.

He had thrown on a long black coat, and it flapped against the wind. He had pulled its large hood tight to shield him from the rain. From the darkness of the hood his eyes were gleaming out like two sinister moons.

He cried, 'That rope there – bring it!' Amy ran to fetch a length of rope that was coiled beside a barn.

'Stand well back from the edge – I need no more of you to fall in with your friend.'

Franklin braced himself against the wind and gazed into the pit with mocking, heartless eyes. So scathing was his look that Caroline's blood ran cold. He made her feel as if she was wholly worthless. She felt herself to be a meaningless creature, trapped by a hungry predator. She said, 'I'm sorry – I missed my footing.'

'Sorry?' said Franklin. 'I'm sure you are.' His scornful voice managed to pierce the roaring wind. 'As sorry as can ever be. Sorry you came. Sorry you were born. Sorry sorry sorry on a shoestring.' But then the old man straightened and appeared to shake off his gloomy air. He fashioned one end of the rope into a clumsy loop. He lowered it to Caroline and said, 'Hook your foot in that. Your friends can haul you up.'

Then Franklin stepped back and handed the trailing end of the rope to the girls, saying, 'You can raise her. I'll not risk my back.'

The three girls tightened the slack, braced their feet in the mud and, with a bit of grunting, a bit of muttering, a bit of complaining, a lot of criticizing, a degree of heroics, and some self-congratulation, they managed to pull Caroline up.

As the sodden group retraced its steps to the rear door of the house, the old man said, 'Mark this lesson well. There are many dangers surrounding Gehenna – dangers far more severe than a fall into a pit. If you'll heed my advice, you will stay close to the house and not wander too far. Do as I tell you and go only where I say. The next time trouble calls I may not be around.'

'There won't be a next time,' Caroline said crossly.

'I wish I could feel so sure … '

10

They formed a sorry bunch, cleaning themselves off by the log-burning range in the kitchen. There was no bathroom in Gehenna; all the water had to be heated in pans, where it produced a peaty scum. Franklin had given them towels, but they were so grubby Lou went to fetch their own.

As she was running back with them from the barn where they'd left their things, she happened to glance up towards Gehenna's roof. In one of the highest windows she thought she saw a face, peering blankly down at her.

It wasn't Franklin's, he had gone down to the cellar. It could not be Martha's; Franklin had explained how she 'can't climb these steep stairs'.

Maybe it wasn't there. Maybe it was a flash of reflected lightning.

Lou told the others, but they weren't that curious. They had enough problems trying to dry off their clothes.

Their entire holiday had rapidly become one long waking nightmare.

And how dull Gehenna was. And how gloomy were the hours they spent in it that day.

The girls were so dispirited that they simply sat around, watching the old couple going about their work: chopping up hunks of meat, lugging great lengths of wood to the 'labyrinth' below.

There were a lot of banging sounds rising through the floor. Franklin was working hard down there. Raising a din.

He was absent several hours. When he eventually re-emerged he seemed pleased with the results.

* * *

'So – what? Should we go to bed?' said Jade, as the time advanced into late evening. 'We've had our supper, we've done the washing-up. We've shrunk our brains with Franklin's pack of cards. At least while we're asleep the boredom goes away and the storm might pass. Maybe tomorrow we can set off for Blacktor.'

'I really hope so, Jade,' Caroline said gloomily. 'It feels as though we've been here for weeks. And it sometimes feels like we'll be lucky to leave.'

So soon after nine o' clock – bored, low and thoroughly depressed – the girls retired to the barn. They took an old brass lantern, for the barn had no lighting. The lamp gave out a meagre glow, and fumed like a funeral pyre. They hung it from a beam as far away from the straw as common sense required. They didn't hang around then, but banged the wide doors shut, dived quickly into bed and pulled their sleeping bags tight. Hoping to keep out bugs. Frightened there might be rats. Pleading for nothing worse.

After a time pure darkness ruled, for the lamp used up its fuel and its pale glow died away. At least for three of the girls that was not a great problem – they had fallen asleep quickly, worn-out by the boring day. It was only Caroline who remained stubbornly awake: turning, yawning, completely fed up. It seemed this was her day for having things go wrong, for suffering bad luck.

She had tried shuffling sideways into softer, deeper straw. But that proved no help at all – sleep refused to respond.

And outside, the raging storm – which had howled away all day – began howling twice as loud.

How could she get to sleep now, while that dreadful din was shattering the night?

She could see bolts of lightning through the gaps in the leaking walls, could feel tremors in the ground as the gun-like thunder roared. She counted the intervals in-between until there were no intervals left to count – for the storm's heart was right above.

Then – as she listened to that remorseless hammering – she was suddenly able just to make out a softer, closer sound. That of something on the roof. Something which picked its way across the old, cracked timber. Something with stealth on its mind.

For a long time Caroline made no move – convinced she must have been mistaken – almost praying that she was. For what could be up there on a night as bad as that? What on earth would creep about like a stalker overhead? If she should sneak outside and risk a look up, what terrible sight might she see silhouetted there?

Her mind was in turmoil – this must surely be a dream.

Why had her body stiffened, become unable to move?

Was she being paralysed by fear? Was she ...

She tried to scream. But not one peep emerged. Soon a cold heavy sweat was streaming out of her and soaking the sleeping bag.

She had become far too frightened to try another scream. A scream might be the key to unlock awful doors. Once the doors had been opened, who knew what terrible things might charge in from the night?

If she could simply lie there, motionless, not breathing – perhaps whatever crawled on the roof might blithely pass her by.

She might be overlooked.

The hunter might not see her, insensible with fear.

But of course that never works. The hunter always sees. The nightmare always comes.

Directly overhead, the stealthy movements ceased. Caroline pictured evil eyes peering down from the roof. Eyes which could pierce the gloom as easily as knives cut through blocks of butter.

There was no hiding place – no shelter but the thin and flimsy quilted bag in which she had to wait.

Wait, while just above a loose board squeaked and creaked as the hunter prised it up.

As if carefully planned, several events suddenly occurred in rapid succession.

Caroline gave a wild lurch, to force herself to act. She found the power to shriek and woke up the other three. A spear of lightning plunged into the yard outside and set a shrub alight.

There was, too, a great gust of wind which tore a branch from a decrepit tree and smashed it down on the roof. When a ragged hole appeared, a figure could be seen, framed by the livid sky.

In an instant of bedlam, part of the roof collapsed. Caroline scrambled to one side as a timber hurtled down. The other girls panicked – their minds still half asleep – caught wholly by surprise.

And the figure plummeted from the roof and landed in straw. Caroline saw blazing eyes in a gaunt and corpse-like face. All this by a lightning flash – and then the flash was gone – and darkness returned. But someone sprinted across the startled barn. Battled to free the doors, then ran out into the night.

'Did you see him?' Caroline cried.

'See who?' Amy replied. 'I can't see a thing in here!'

11

Almost as startling as those few bizarre moments was the arrival of Franklin. Within mere moments he was bursting through the doors, holding a lamp aloft, his long black coat flapping and streaming out behind him. Light from the burning shrub framed him in glory while, up above, the storm shrieked to its peak.

'What's going on?' he cried.

'Someone came through the roof!'

'*What?*' Franklin's face turned upwards; his eyes probed the gloom. The wind which gripped his coat made it crack like a sail. Water streamed down his face.

'There's no one here!' he cried. 'A rotting branch broke away. It crashed down through the roof – you are lucky nobody was killed! But there's no one in here – only a pile of twigs. What nonsense, what drivel, what rubbish you create!'

After a few moments, Franklin added, 'But there is no point in your remaining here with that rain pouring in – you would be best advised to sleep in the house. You can make up some beds in one of the upstairs rooms.' Franklin lowered the guttering lamp, turned its light onto the girls. Their shocked faces were taut. His own looked grey and pinched. But his mocking eyes blazed. 'Or would you rather stay out here in the rain, with your mystery prowler?'

The girls gathered their things, followed him from the barn.

They trailed him through the mud towards Gehenna's porch.

Once inside, he slammed the door.

'Take these,' he said brusquely, as he thrust a pile of bedding into Caroline's arms. 'Go to the first room you come to, up the stairs. Take these candles with you; there is no lighting up there. You will find matches in the hall. Can you manage all that or might the house burn down?'

'Look, Mr Franklin – '

'Just Franklin,' he muttered.

'I really saw someone!'

'So you keep telling me.'

Caroline bit down on her tongue and stalked back to her waiting friends.

She said, 'He thinks I'm a liar.'

12

Caroline quickly discovered that Franklin was not the only one harbouring some doubts. None of her friends had seen the figure in the barn. They wondered if she had, possibly, maybe got it wrong. Amidst all the chaos – the dust and noise and falling branches – perhaps she'd been confused. 'It was so dark,' said Lou, 'and you were half asleep. I'm sure you saw *something* - but not a 'wild-eyed man'. Maybe a piece of felt or lining from the roof. Which might, in the moment, look like a man.'

Caroline said, 'Don't try to humour me – I know what men look like. He was wearing a long black coat, like the one Franklin had on. But a whole lot baggier and streaming out behind so that it helped to slow his fall. I really saw him!'

'If only we had too.'

'Well don't blame me for *that* – I was the only one awake!'

The others shuffled and mumbled, reluctant to say more. But their glances spoke volumes.

After a time, Caroline walked away, angered that she had not received better trust and support. It was not her fault that no one else had seen. She knew in her own head that she'd not been deceived. Inside the midnight barn she had seen a black-clothed man framed by the fiery sky.

She could still picture him as clear as day in her mind. His dull staring eyes, his pale hair, sallow skin. Though not like normal skin: more like old parchment that had wrinkled and been bleached by lime.

She could imagine, too, how such skin would be formed. It would be formed in gloom, in rooms shunned by sunlight. Prisoners in deep dungeons would surely develop such skin, given sufficient time.

While Caroline wandered restlessly down the stairs, the others made their beds up in their draughty room. It was a bitterly cold place, crypt-like, with wooden walls. The ceiling had been carved into figures like gargoyles. Small, grotesque faces watched them, checking on every move that the weary girls made.

They watched them spreading sheets on four-poster beds fashioned from wood so heavy the legs had dented the floorboards. They watched them stir the drapes which hung around the beds, making them flutter like ghosts.

But oh, that cold, though: no source of power served the upper floors. Candles and small log fires did what they could. But nothing was a match for that cold.

13

As Caroline reached the quiet ground floor she thought she saw a tapestry move, as if disturbed by wind. There was no wind, though: the hallway was quite still. Curiosity made her move, sylph-like, across the floor. She raised one frayed edge of the cloth, and was surprised to find a tiny room beyond.

It was like a prison cell, which may have served some use in former darker times, but was redundant now. All that the room contained was one small wooden stool, a candle and a chair.

And one slight figure – Franklin, clutching a bone. A bone which appeared to have been freshly torn from the chest of a slaughtered beast. Strands of fat and raw meat were hanging from his lips. 'My supper,' he murmured slyly.

* * *

'I think we've upset Caroline,' Lou said, as she leaned across her bed to tuck threadbare blankets in. 'I'll make her bed up, to show her we're still friends.'

Jade walked across the room to lend a helping hand. At every step she felt herself watched by the eyes of the ceiling carvings. 'She won't fret for long, though – she's not the sulking sort. We're all edgy and tense because we're hungry and tired.' Jade smoothed Caroline's mattress down. It was as cold as ice. As was all the bedding.

'It's also possible, of course, that Caroline was right. Maybe there was someone, and we were just too slow to see him.' Jade plumped down heavily on the edge of the half-made bed, and punched a lumpy bolster straight.

'In fact, the one thing that can be said for sure – and I assume I'm speaking for everyone here – is that all we've achieved on our jolly-fun-jaunt is the remarkable feat of getting ourselves trapped in a creepy old house - with a couple of people who frighten the hell out of us!'

But, creepy old house or not, the girls were so worn-out their worries had to wait. As soon as Caroline returned to the room they all clambered into bed. Blew out the candles – except for a small one which gave sufficient light to take the sinister edge off the oppressive place. At least, it tried to; but as with so many things, there was a downside to each advantage gained. For the murky flickering light made the carved shapes overhead appear to be shifting and moving at times. As if they were alive …

14

At some point in the night, as if by a miracle, the storm blew itself out. But in its aftermath sinister forms appeared: spectral shapes from the earth – mist-ghosts, eerily pale; tendrils of drifting fog combining and coalescing into impenetrable banks.

By the time dawn came and its dim light managed to tease the girls awake, the temperature had plummeted by more than ten degrees. The moorland landscape showed the first glimmers of frost. Black birds were shivering in exposed trees.

Indeed, so much change occurred within those few short hours that it appeared as if life itself had been moved, transported to a different world. The change was so dramatic, so sudden and so wide-reaching, that it almost seemed to be supernatural.

'Holy magombas,' Amy whispered, as she gazed out on a scene of near-mystical aspect. A still, grey ocean extended all around the house. Barns appeared as derelict ships, each one hopelessly becalmed. Walls, fence posts, shrubs and trees – abandoned machinery – forgotten implements – were like dead hulks wallowing on a doldrum tide. The sight reached into Amy's soul and made everything sink inside. She said, 'It's all been changed. The landscape is transformed. There is nothing to be seen now but fog.'

The others moved to join Amy at the long, bowed window which overlooked the yard.

One glance confirmed to them that the world they had known was gone. Outside they would be as lost as newborn puppies. They would be crushed by the weight of silence and stillness, like a group of ants squashed inside a fist.

Also, there is no known sound which can best the wiles of fog. No air is as suppressing as that absorbing vaporous veil. No threat feels quite so near as the one that may come creeping up, concealed inside fog's cloak …

'Dear me,' Franklin murmured, having arrived without a sound at the doorway of the room. 'How terrible it is that things have changed so dramatically, and yet you still find yourselves trapped. As fast as the tempest disappeared, so hope fades in your breasts. In these parts a fog may persist for several days. It has been known to last for weeks. Who can ever tell? And this one is a real pea-souper!'

Franklin cackled like a hag. The girls stared numbly back, not sure how to react. The look on Franklin's face was ecstatic.

There was, though, no alternative other than to spend at least another day in the discomforting company of their hosts.

In truth, it was mainly Franklin whom the girls had contact with. Martha was rarely seen – she usually stayed in her room. Whether this was through nervousness or a distrust of visitors was never quite made clear.

The girls strained to miss her, though, for on the occasions she did appear she would often giggle alarmingly, in the manner of a crazed baboon. She suffered from uncontrolled giggling – as if, concealed inside her bulk, there lurked an unhinged soul.

'I still prefer her to Franklin, though,' Caroline said, as she later helped to clear away the breakfast things. She was having enormous difficulty shaking the old man from her mind. The image from last night constantly intruded on her thoughts. The memory of his teeth as he pulled on the meat, the spittle on his chin. An almost primitive delight had filled his eyes: a gleam of lustful joy from wolfing blood-rich meat. Meat so glutted with blood it stained his fingers red, and dribbled on the floor.

Even the slam-bang and clattering of pans could not suppress a fear that the old pair might be insane. Rational, mortal souls don't gorge upon raw flesh – nor toil like human moles.

'And they've both been underground,' Jade said. 'I heard the pair of them digging below. Have you looked at their fingers? They've been cut right to the bone. All their nails have ripped away, and what's underneath is raw. What skin's left on their hands is barely clinging on – it's just transparent flaps. I really can't stand much more of this. I'm going to have to leave.' She paused to wipe the grease and grime from her hands. 'I honestly can't take it, I really can't. I'll go completely nuts if I hang around this place.' Which was understandable, and its sentiment entirely reasonable: but did overlook the impassable weather on the moor.

Lou said, 'That's risky, Jade. How far do you think you're likely to get? You heard what Franklin said.'

Jade said, ' I don't care any more. The only thing I know is that I can't stay here, I'm getting too upset. The aura's really bad. I don't know about the rest of you but I'm going to head for Blacktor.'

This idea also appealed to Amy, although she had a fear of fog – a phobia which stretched back almost thirteen years. (As a small child she had once been trapped on a cliff by dense sea mist and had been rigid for hours. Her father had to come to pluck her to safety.) 'What do you think, Lou – should we trying leaving too?'

Lou gave an anxious shrug. 'It's too risky. I'm not sure.'

'We've got the compass … ' said Jade.

'A lot of help that was before: it was that which brought us here. I'm just not certain … ' Lou's face twisted with doubt. She looked almost in pain, so confused was her mind.

'What about you, Caroline?' said Jade. 'Do you want to give it a try?'

Caroline agreed without hesitation. Caroline had already seen too much.

As the girls had wandered some distance from the area covered by their own map, they needed to enquire whether Franklin had one they could borrow. This request was assigned to Caroline, who gloomily observed that for most of the unappealing tasks the matter of her greater age inevitably came into play. There were some drawbacks to being the group's eldest, and they weren't always immediately apparent.

But she accepted the view that possessing a faint heart never won anyone any maps, so she girded her loins and tracked down the old man, who was cleaning off tools in a utility room.

She said, 'I'm sorry to ask – and I'm sorry to disturb you - but would you have a map of the surrounding area that we could borrow?'

Franklin took a break from cleaning a muddy spade, and said, 'No doubt I do. Somewhere or other.'

'Two of us are thinking of leaving.'

'In this fog?' he said. 'That is unwise. You would not make twenty yards.'

'We're hoping to reach Blacktor.'

'Blacktor!' Franklin looked horrified. 'Blacktor's twelve miles away!'

'I know,' said Caroline. 'We'll need to move. We hope to get there before it's dark.'

'It isn't the darkness, child – it's the weather you should fear. These moors become death traps. People disappear … '

But the old man paused. He seemed to give the matter some thought, then gestured with his palms, and let his shoulders shrug. As though he'd done his best. Had tried to talk sense into inexperienced minds.

He said, 'It is a fool's errand and you have little idea of what awaits you outside. But I recognize the fact that it is not my place to compel you to stay. So if you will wait yourselves here, I shall fetch you a map.'

* * *

Supplied with a faded and greatly tattered map, Caroline went to find Jade, and the pair hurried to their room. They lit two sputtering candles for their gloomy room was permanently choked with some murk. They spread the old map on a bed, bent over it and pored, looking for something to give them hope. After a while Jade said, 'Going back the way we came would only end us up on that pretty rough track. A shorter route would be along this footpath - ' She pointed to a serpentine design of dots and lines. 'That cuts this whole corner off, and could save us a lot of time.'

'And also get us lost.' Caroline pulled a face. The line went meandering through a marked bog. She said, 'After so much rain that bog might be a swamp.'

'But the footpath's clearly highlighted on the map, so it must be fit to walk. And it could take us two hours less.'

'I guess,' said Caroline, not overly enthused. 'It's just that the major lanes are more likely to be clear.'

'But we don't have all that much time to spare,' said Jade. 'We have to make a lot of distance before it gets dark. Because either way we're going to get stuffed if it gets dark.'

So the decision was made to take the old footpath that wound through Harold's Bog. With the hope that old Harold was in one of his good moods.

The girls gathered the few things they would take. A plastic covering for the map, Jade's torch, a change of clothes. They intended to travel light, planning to reach Blacktor before needing supplies.

They were unusually silent, for both of them were tense. But there was some comfort to be found in being active at last. They had been depressed for far too long by the ambience and spite of that dark morbid house.

By the time the pair were ready to leave the day was approaching noon: they would be cutting things fine. Even then they found themselves obliged to pause for a while, for when they opened Gehenna's door the very pressure of the fog was like a punch to their chests. They had never seen such a fog. Had never witnessed such opacity. They had never before inhaled such a dank air into their lungs.

The fog had been discontented by simply covering the landscape, and had gone on to completely obscure the sky so that it seemed the whole world was enveloped by twilight. It muffled every sound. It played tricks on the eyes. It tried to push through the doorway as if it had a plan.

'Caroline … ' Jade murmured. 'Are we sure that this is probably the right thing to do?'

'Come on, Jade - this was your idea. Don't go changing your mind now that I've agreed to go. It's only fog. It's not like the Apocalypse. How much harm can we seriously come to? At the end of the day it's just murky air. All we need to do is find the path.'

'I suppose you're right,' said Jade.

'The worst thing that can happen to us is that we fall in a bog.'

'You're right,' said Jade.

'So all things considered – taking it all into account – it's best if you go first … '

* * *

The pair said a quick goodbye to Louisa and Amy. The old couple were not around.

'We'll send some help back,' said Caroline.

'You'd better,' muttered Lou.

'Keep the flag flying here.'

'Bravely. Don't lose your path.'

'Jade's got it all marked out. It should take us about six hours, assuming we don't end up lost.'

'You've got the compass?'

'It's hanging round my neck.'

'And you've a few dry clothes?'

'Lou – you're worse than my mum.'

'And have you checked your torch?'

'Yes, Lou, it's been checked. It still looks like a torch.'

The girls stepped outside the door and at once a bitterly cold air wrapped its hands around their throats. Their grey breath streamed out, had seizures, disappeared. The first pinpricks of frost needled against their skin. Ice sparkled in the air like the eyes of tiny ghosts whose empire was dissolving around them.

'I can't even see the gates, Jade – this fog is impenetrable!'

'Stick by me, Caroline – hold my hand, we'll be all right!'

To the sisters in the doorway – watching with anxious eyes – their plucky friends vanished all too soon …

15

As bad as the fog appeared, it barely hinted at the problems it was going to present. The earth beneath it was a glutinous morass of decaying plant life, surface water and diluvial mud. The saturated moor was, for much of its breadth, a continuous swamp. So sodden was the land that it was impossible to tell where the firmer ground ended and Harold's Bog began. It was as if the bog had spread until its cold black paws were clawing right at Gehenna's walls.

'Any sign of the path?'

'I'm hoping we're on it,' said Jade. 'The ground feels fairly solid. As long as we don't go in too far above our knees – '

'*Our knees?*' Caroline squawked. 'What's wrong with just our feet?'

'All right. As long as we can see at least part of our feet – then we should be okay … '

That demarcation line had to be swiftly compromised, or all progress would have ceased. The girls could not take more than a few cautious steps without floundering in pools or slick-slimy puddles, teetering on the brink of falling over. The wild moor was restless, organic, and seemingly possessed of what appeared to be a streak of almost sentient spite. Its greatest single joy seemed to lie in its ability to make people fall into its squelching traps.

Yet they still battled on – bravely or foolishly: at times they weren't sure which. They forgot all their plans, their intentions and their objective – all they could focus on was trying to locate an area of land which at the least might accommodate their weight. Wet cold and clumsy, they felt as though their wills were being absorbed by the quagmire – until they could barely recognize where their tired bodies ended and the claims of raw nature began.

As they struggled on, their minds muddled by swamp gas and their vision by haziness, a bizarre thing began occurring around them. Huge swarms of insects which thrived on the moorland sludge began to emit shimmering pulses of light as the pair passed. An eerie phosphorescence emerged from the creatures, and as the girls moved forward they left in their wake a trail of pallid green light – a spectral causeway snaking back through the swamp.

They toiled for an hour - failed to make much progress – and then were jolted by a scream close at hand.

Caroline snatched at Jade's arm.

'*What the eff was that?*'

'Probably a deer,' said Jade, without much conviction.

'Do deer actually scream?'

'Maybe it's a fox.'

'Do they scream? Do foxes let out screams?'

'I don't know! Ask a fox!'

'You're not being a great help at the moment.'

Barely had that fright passed when they heard a second noise – something less distinct than the scream. It was a stealthy and sinister splashing sound - as if something was matching them, parallel to their course. Something out in the swamp. Something large enough to produce ripples which lapped over the path.

The girls stood motionless, straining to locate the source. Both of them ran through a list of suspects in their minds: livestock, a deer, a pony, an otter. Or maybe it was an advancing man -

They paused long enough to be certain of what it was – then they turned tail and ran. A man was out there, stalking them through the swamp. They had glimpsed his dim outline and his breath stirring the fog. And a man in a swamp wasn't good news.

It couldn't be too far back to Gehenna - their progress had been pitifully slow. But how far was it? Close enough to get away - or far enough that they would end up caught?

Could they stick to the path formed by the glimmering bugs?

Could they beat the man from the swamp if it came to a race?

16

'They should be well on their way,' said Amy. 'It must be more than an hour since they left. They might have even cleared the fog. I'm starting to think that maybe it wasn't a good idea to stay behind.'

'You could be right,' Lou said, fixing a frown. 'It seems sort of silly now – I don't suppose there's much that can really go too wrong. My trouble is that I worry too much.'

'It's a pity you can't learn to relax. Someone like Caroline is very laid-back. You should try to be more like her.'

'I – ' Lou's head swivelled round. 'Did you hear that?' she said.

'What?' said Amy.

'It sounded like somebody screamed!'

The sisters hurried from the kitchen, through the long, gloomy hallway. They wrenched the front door open.

Outside, the fog lay more thickly than before, so dense had it become that it looked as solid as a wall. Even Gehenna's steps – a mere arm's-length away – were invisible.

The crushing silence in the yard was so profound that it seemed impossible for a lone voice to survive.

But a voice called out again, with a thin, terrified scream.

Nearer now, and closing …

Caroline staggered from the fog with Jade right on her heels. They stumbled up the wide grey steps. They pushed the sisters backwards into the entrance hall. Bolted the heavy door; made sure it was secure. Leaned their shoulders on it – panting, pallid and taut.

'What's going on?' cried Lou.

'Someone came after us,' said Jade, fighting for breath. 'A man out of the swamp – chased us right back to the house.'

'Is he still outside now?'

As if in answer, someone thumped on the door!

The frightened girls backed off as a fusillade of blows descended on the wood. They were powered by such force that the whole doorframe shook. Ancient oak panels creaked, black gloss paint peeled and flaked. Old hinges protested, straining against their screws as if trying to escape. When the first salvo of fury produced no obvious result, the hammering intensified – fuelled by both fists and feet.

Plaster dust trickled down from the grey wall above. Splinters cracked from the wood.

But, as is the way of things, everything passes; nothing endures for too long. After several terrified moments the hammering subsided. To be replaced by something much much worse – a prolonged and ominous silence. A silence so intense that it appeared to snuff out every move and thought. The girls were rigid, they forgot how to inhale. Their hearts forgot to beat, clear thinking all but ceased. All they could do was stare, horrified, at the door and wonder what would come next ...

'Perhaps he's gone,' Lou whispered.

'I doubt it,' muttered Jade. 'He'll be planning his next move. He can't get through here, so he'll go – '

'Round the back!' The words leapt from Amy's mouth and fresh fear filled her eyes. 'Has the kitchen door been locked?'

'It's never been locked before.'

Terror took on a new face ...

They ran like scared rabbits playing a crazy game of catch-me-if-you-can. All of them sprinting, with Amy in the lead. They pounded through long pools of shade, past brooding rooms and echoing niches. They thundered along the hall with every muscle strained, their hearts wildly pumping, their limbs feeling almost on fire.

But in the kitchen things altered and they skidded to a halt. The rear door stood ajar and mist rolled in from outside.

And damp footprints on the floor showed where someone had entered ...

The line of prints progressed towards a second door – a storeroom they presumed. They had seen Franklin enter it carrying tools and logs. They'd not been inside themselves as they'd had no cause before. But that was set to change: having advanced this far they could not back down now.

Caroline – strong and fit, worked out at a gym – snatched a long weighty stake from a wood pile by the hearth.

With knuckles blanching, she advanced towards the door. Her eyes were fierce and bright, her lips were thin and tight. Pennons of frightened breath fluttered between her teeth, which she was grinding so hard she made them ache.

She said to Amy, 'Open it. Lift the latch.'

Amy said, 'I'm too scared.'

'Do it, Amy!' Caroline said.

She raised the stake aloft, ready to pound someone.

But suddenly the door thundered open …

* * *

'What's this?' Franklin exclaimed as he burst out of the room, thrusting the girls aside as he moved.

'We've got an intruder!' cried Amy.

'In the house?' Franklin's voice changed in tone – became a snake-like hiss. 'There's no intruder here. What nonsense!'

'Look down there!' said Amy. 'Fresh footprints!'

Franklin merely grunted. 'Those footprints are mine,' he said. 'I've been outside. I had to go across the yard to fetch more dry logs. I store them in that room. Good grief!' He hurried off, leaving dark, damp footprints – and the four girls wondering.

Had Franklin followed Caroline and Jade onto the moor, then chivvied them back? Was there a reason why they weren't supposed to leave? Had he pounded on the door just to frighten them some more and ensure they stayed inside?

What was his purpose? What could he hope to gain? Or had he told the truth, and there was still someone else outside?

Either option seemed grim, and the questions they proposed offered no easy answers.

17

Despite all that had occurred the situation remained the same: the girls were still virtual prisoners. Everything conspired against them, keeping them at the house. All that they tried seemed destined to fall flat. They were far from help, with no ending in sight, and a stack of worries that were only piling higher. Their only bright spot revolved around the building of a fire, when the gloom of evening spread like a bruise through the girls' bedroom. The cheerful crackling of the logs brought them some warmth and cheer: but all too soon the flames died down.

'I'll ask Franklin for some more logs,' said Amy, as a piercing chill crept swiftly through the room.

'Want me to come with you?' said Lou, who wasn't keen on the four of them splitting up. She thought they should remain close. Too many creepy things had happened, so much trauma and tension had occurred. And she'd seen a lot of horror films.

'No – I'll be okay,' said Amy, who perhaps, being the least serious in nature of the girls, was the one best equipped for bouncing back again from doubts and setbacks. She was straightforward and easy: simple in her heart. She could plunge to the depths, then soar back to the heights. Tragedy would be a flaring spot on her chin; ecstasy was a smile from somebody she liked.

She trotted down the stairs, tracked by dark, leering looks from grotesquely carved reliefs. The ancient oak panelling which lined Gehenna's walls had been intricately worked into totems and gargoyles: images so lifelike that one could well believe real flesh had somehow been monstrously sealed inside the wood. Demons and furies were gazing out of nooks: exotic beings waged pitched battles for the stairs. And now, alone, it suddenly dawned on Amy that their malevolent eyes seemed to move – watching and monitoring her every step.

'Franklin?' Amy called three times but if the old man heard he was not in a mood for replying. Her somewhat forlorn voice was swallowed by a pool of silence so intense that even her own breathing seemed to roar in her ears. The rustle of her clothing – the creaking of floorboards – were sounds which issued right along the hall. She called out, 'Martha!' but still nobody replied. There was an echoing empty feel to the entire gloomy house.

At that late hour, with the house shrouded in fog, the very world itself felt extinct.

Amy remained in the hall, not certain where to look, hoping to catch even the faintest of sounds. She finally heard one – a low, throbbing burr - like the moans of a sick bloodhound inside an abandoned church. Rhythmic and repetitive, it was almost a chant. It caused the floor to vibrate slightly. So close did its source appear that Amy was surprised she'd not heard it before, nor noticed it begin. Somehow it just seemed to be there. Perhaps it always was. Perhaps Gehenna was in a state of perpetual groaning.

The mournful dirge emerged from Martha's room, and was noticeably growing in strength.

As Amy ventured closer to the locked door she could see, around the knotted wood, escaping candle light. The frame had been loosened by warping through the years, and she could just about peer within. She could see nothing clearly, just enough to discern shadows in the room beyond, amorphous outlines, swaying from side to side. There were at least two shadows; maybe more. It was difficult to be certain. The shadows constantly wove and merged.

Certainly there appeared to be two distinct voices. But then Amy heard a flurry of noise from up above – the creaking of a board – the rustle of cloth on the landing overhead. That could surely only be Franklin, and if that was the case his sister must be alone in her room. Amy must have misheard. Or imagined something different.

She moved away from the door and hurried up the stairs, hoping to catch the old man before he disappeared again.

But even as she reached the landing above, she heard the sounds fade away into nothing.

* * *

When half an hour had passed without Amy's return, Lou felt compelled to look for her. Not only was she concerned by the length of time she'd been away, but she'd also heard strange sounds coming from the rooms below. Stealthy, suspicious sounds. Door hinges protesting. Creaks from old floorboards. Though she had been moved to mention this, the others weren't impressed. Both Caroline and Jade were poring over Franklin's map. Seeking another route. A way to clear the swamp. A safer passage by which they could reach Blacktor.

Taking a scarf and coat – for the air had turned dungeon-cold – Lou padded down the stairs. At first the ground floor seemed abandoned; nobody spoke or moved. There was no sign of Amy there, nor of Franklin or Martha. And the only sounds she heard came from a pan of stew which simmered in the unlit kitchen.

But when she reached Gehenna's musty library, she found the frail figure of Franklin, seemingly lost in deep thought. He was standing by the dusty table, perusing a ferociously thick book. A door behind his back leaned fractionally ajar. By the lantern light within, Lou could make it out as a private study.

Lou cleared her throat. 'My sister, Amy – have you seen her?'

Franklin smiled. He did not often smile, and Lou wished he hadn't now. His tongue was thin and black, his few teeth long and sharp and crooked, like a set of faulty dentures for a snake. 'She's not in here,' he said. 'Only my humble self. Plus this fine old book, of course.' He turned it around to show it to her. 'A work which is my family's pride and joy. The records of Gehenna over five hundred years. It's quite valuable, of course, but – so much more than that – it is absolutely and completely irreplaceable. My family's entire history is recorded in this book. More than half a millennium of bloodshed, war and strife. Upset, turmoil and struggle. Death, disease, catastrophe and revival. You are welcome to peruse it, if you wish.'

Lou said, 'Thank you. That's kind of you. It sounds very fascinating. But maybe some other time … '

18

While Lou fretted downstairs, her sister was blundering around almost blindly up above. So vast was the old house, and so intricate its design, that she had abandoned any hope of memorizing a route back: she had simply set her thoughts on eventually catching up with the elusive sounds ahead.

She had pursued them up creaking staircases and through hallways dark as forests. She had called out Franklin's name, but received nothing in reply. Puzzled at first; then indignant; she threw in a mixture of frustration, vexation and generally feeling stumped. But after pursuing him so far, she was determined to succeed.

She never quite saw his figure, though – she always managed to fall one stride too late. How fast that old man could move when he set his mind to it! Why wouldn't he slow down? Why could she never gain on him? It was like trying to catch up with a gust of wind.

At length though, finally, Amy reached what surely had to be the highest tier of the house. If she ascended any further she would get lost in the clouds. If she were able to look straight down she would find herself reeling from vertigo. The door that she had reached must be the one which opened into Gehenna's attic.

The door was narrow and slightly arched, and stood partially open. Lying beyond it was a room illuminated by the eerie yellow half-light produced by a small lantern. Had Franklin gone inside? If he had, he had once again ignored Amy's latest call. Was it mere impatience that had made him race ahead – or was he simply not in a conversational mood? Maybe it was all a game. Perhaps he was teasing her in some way. Franklin's idea of a joke.

Amy crossed the dim threshold. Immediately inside was the flickering paraffin lamp which provided the light. She had certainly arrived at Gehenna's attic all right – there couldn't be any doubt of that. The place sported a rotting and sagging cobwebby roof with mould and slime and patches of exposed plaster, and an expansive colony of small resting bats. There were storage trunks and old tea chests. Old clothes hung from racks. Chairs with missing legs or tattered fabric or collapsed seats. Paintings grey with dust. Mirrors without their lustre. A place for junk that would never find itself salvaged.

And there was the slightest hint of movement – of something there but not seen.

Amy felt no draught in the attic, could detect no movement in the air. But just behind her – without her noticing – the door was swinging shut.

* * *

Lou padded up the stairs, having checked every room that stood unlocked below. Following a sixth sense (or maybe a trace of familiar perfume in the air) she was fairly certain that she was on Amy's trail. Her sister must be up above, though what she sought up there was a mystery to Lou. But that was Amy: mercurial in mood, and prone to change her ideas at the drop of a hat. Her curiosity would be the death of her one day, Lou often thought.

A heavy muffled thud caused Lou to pull up short. A sharp gasp followed behind. She had picked up a cheap wax candle somewhere along the way. By its hesitant light she could just make out a door a little way ahead. A rapid assessment of her position suggested it would be the loft. She started forward and the thud sounded again, with the kind of leaden force that falling bodies make. She broke into a run, yanked open the door –

Amy said, 'Hi there, Lou.'

'I thought you were being attacked,' said Lou, as she practically squirmed with embarrassment.

Amy said, 'Who by?'

'I didn't know,' said Lou. 'All I heard was a thump.'

'I was just shifting this trunk. There's another room back there – I was trying to clear some space so I could clamber through. You frightened the life out of me!'

'I was only trying to help.'

'Then you can help me now. Drag out those other crates. And bring that lamp nearer. You worry too much, Lou. You need to loosen up.'

The two girls eased their way through veils of grey cobwebs, guided by the small lamp. Extending ahead of them was a narrow, low-roofed room. Its walls were naked brick, completely unadorned. Its floor was unplaned wood, so splintered and decayed that it would rasp off flesh. There were no windows, no brackets to hold lamps. No hint that the room was used for anything but junk. And yet what junk there was. A veritable treasure trove of junk. Junk to startle the most jaded of eyes …

They picked their wary past tables chock-a-block with relics and antiques. Cracked leather tunics jostled to find a space among stout hiking boots, rucksacks and parchment maps. Walking sticks leaned in rows, their ranks increased by riding crops and crooks. Oilskins and greatcoats spilled out of crates and chests; saddles and riding tack hid watches, flasks and keys; whistles dangled from chains; earrings were heaped on coins; binoculars and combs …

At first bafflingly diverse, with a little study the stacked goods revealed a common link. Most of the items were connected to hiking or riding: the everyday objects that careless walkers or riders might casually leave behind. Or misplace in a storm, or lose in long grass, or have stolen from them in the dead of night. There was also an uncomfortably intimate feel about the whole display, as if the owners hoped one day to claim it back. For surely there must be owners? There was far too much for the old couple's use …

Lou said, 'We ought to leave. This is a private room and we shouldn't be here. Stick to the main rooms – that's what Franklin advised.'

'He also told us we were free to look around. Besides, he led me here.'

'He can't have done, he's downstairs.'

'Well someone showed the way. At least, they seemed to – ' Amy said uncertainly. 'It was hard to tell sometimes if they were there or not. Just rustles and shadows. Maybe it was the wind.'

'Amy, there is no wind. It was just your imagination.'

With the mystery unresolved – but still in need of logs – the sisters made their way back downstairs. Franklin apparently had not ventured from Gehenna's library. He said, 'More logs, is it?' when the girls made their request. 'More wood to keep you warm? Aye, there's no harm in that – we've wood enough to spare.'

He put his precious book down.

'There is wood inside and out. Some good logs in the yard, but they're too wet to use. You'll want the drier ones. The best are kept downstairs, just inside the cellar.'

After their adventures in the loft, the last thing the girls desired was a late-night trip below. 'We needn't go, need we?' said Amy.

Franklin sighed. 'Do you think the logs you need will march themselves up the stairs? You're not nervous, are you?'

'Not much,' Amy muttered.

'Good. You can lend a hand.'

Reluctantly they followed Franklin from the library, through the hallway and down the steps to the cellar. He lit a lantern and its thin yellow rays probed ahead. The light revealed a lumber room with a wide archway set in one wall. Beyond lay such a tract of darkness as the girls had not dreamed of before. Absolute darkness, more solid than a rock. A darkness so intense it almost crushed the lantern's light. A darkness which seemed complete, yet merely marked the beginning of a vast labyrinth of gloom.

Walking right at his heels, the sisters tracked the old man through the imposing arch. Past soot-streaked wall lamps, which Franklin left unlit, seemingly content to trust in his guttering lantern. The girls were not so sure; they were of the view that floodlights should be employed. They felt almost smothered by the pressure in the shafts, by the tonnes of rock and earth that closed in all around. Numbed by the bitter cold. Choked by the noxious smell. A smell born of decay.

'We once had foxes down here,' Franklin growled through his teeth. 'They burrowed through from the yard. I put down poison, but a few may have survived. That's probably what makes the smell, they leave lumps of rotting food behind. Tough bones and clumps of fur, droppings and dead rabbits. Be careful of where you plant your feet.'

After a brief silent walk Franklin pointed towards a towering pile of wood. 'I store it here because the earlier passage sometimes floods.'

The wood pile was formed from well-seasoned fence posts that he'd been using for supports: the tunnels walls were weak and in need of constant shoring up. The entire labyrinth gave the feeling of something on the brink of collapsing into dust.

Maybe that was why Franklin so often toiled there. Maybe he was afraid that one day his whole house would end up in the earth. Although - if that was the case, why did he also labour maniacally to excavate fresh shafts? Was Franklin looking for something, or had he worked so long down there he'd simply run out of control? Maybe he'd fashioned a plan to burrow right to the earth's core ... It would be impossible to fathom the old man's goal.

While Lou was gathering logs, she noticed that Franklin's gaze had fixed on a distant point.

She straightened slowly, to join him in his search. What was he looking at with such intense fervour? Lou could see only gloom, could hear only the trickle of water some distance off.

But, for an instant, she had a disquieting sense that they were not alone, that their small group was being observed. She tried to shake the feeling off as Franklin turned away and slowly lowered his fuming lantern.

'Nothing down there,' he said. 'Nothing to interest you. Stick with the task you've got. Only the tunnels, the darkness and the rats. No reason to explore – at least, not on this night. It's still not quite ready yet.'

'Ready?' Lou asked nervously.

'Aye,' he said. 'There are still things to do ... '

19

With more than sufficient logs to last them through the night, the girls made their way back upstairs. They dropped the logs in the room's vast hearth. Stacked four on the flames, which now glowed soft and low. Blew gently until the fresh wood hissed and smoked and began to spark. Then they related their tale.

They said the attic was like a 'hikers museum'. The cellar down below was like 'a pillaged tomb'. 'And Franklin's getting ever more weird – he's started seeing things that no one else can see.'

But it all sounded different in the company of friends: the sinister edges frayed as humour forced its way in. Few things mellow people as much as the flames of a warming fire; few sounds are more homely. In fact so homely was the room that, when the fire took hold, the four girls began to slump. Their tensions faded and tiredness soothed their minds. Their eyelids felt like lead and their limbs like bars of iron. One by one they sloped off, clambered onto their beds, pulled their sheets tight, settled down.

To the sound of applewood crackling in the hearth – a sound like cannons discharging in a war amongst fairies – they drifted into sleep, hoping that for tonight at least they would be able to enjoy some decent dreams …

* * *

Soon, though, a dreadful hammering shook the locked front door, jerking the girls awake. At once their startled minds raced back to the failed trek through the swamp. Perhaps Jade had got it wrong; perhaps there was someone. Not Franklin – somebody else: someone who lurked in the swamp and now had returned to snatch them from their beds.

It was late into the night and the fire had burned low. All the candles had died out and they tried but failed to relight one. The girls had to get dressed by the frosty aura given off by the fog.

They crept to the top of the stairs. as tense as a group of thieves on their maiden outing. All their senses were twitching. Down below, Franklin was advancing on the door. They heard his slippered feet padding along the hall. They heard him throw the bolts and yank the heavy door back. It scraped on marble slabs. And then came his voice, querulous as a dog dragged away from a bone. 'This is somebody's home! You can't come banging on doors in the middle of the night!'

'I'm sorry it's so late.'

That voice was younger, softer. Was it a threat? Was that the kind of voice a psychopath might possess?

The girls looked at each other. Would Franklin let him in? And, if he did – what then?

The new voice came from the hallway.

'My pickup slid into a ditch while I was checking stock.'

'At this hour?' said Franklin.

'It wasn't from choice. My employer sent me out – it wasn't my idea. I work at Wellbeck Farm, you know? A bit beyond the ridge.'

'Wellbeck Farm is miles away. You've no stock out this way. And what is *that* foul thing?'

'That's my dog, Jess, sir.'

'It looks like a rabid wolf. Is that animal trained?'

'She's more harmless than she looks.'

'And what's that at your side?'

'My shotgun,' said the voice. 'I didn't want to leave it on the moor … '

The pair of voices trailed away as Franklin and the newcomer proceeded along the hall. The girls crept downstairs with Caroline in the lead. They crouched outside the kitchen door, listening hard. But failed to quite make out what was being discussed.

'Why don't you all come in?'

The voice was Franklin's – he'd whipped the door open. He was dressed in a long torn gown of brown and black brocade. His grey hair was a mess, like a nest thrown together by a blind bird.

'We have a visitor,' he growled, using a tone not unfamiliar to those who had heard him speak before. 'A stranger from the night. He is hoping I'll pity him!'

The visitor's dog snarled.

While the girls hovered awkwardly in the doorway of the room, the stranger's gaze swept over them. He was as sleek and handsome as a young, freshly groomed fox. His eyes were midnight blue, set in a lean, tanned face. Hair like a raven's wing, fluttering in the breeze of every movement he produced.

He stared at Caroline. 'I nearly died out there!'

She felt she was transfixed. Redness seeped through her skin. She whispered, 'I'm sorry.'

The stranger gave a shrug, leaned down to pat his dog, let his breath whistle out.

'But this guy won't believe me – he thinks I'm some kind of thief. Come to steal all his gold … '

'Have you?'

The young man laughed.

He stared right into her eyes, as if probing her soul. Softly he murmured, 'What do you think?'

20

To satisfy the girls' curiosity, the new arrival ran through his whole tale again. It seemed that his name was Daniel; the youngest of the hands employed on Wellbeck Farm, a dozen kilometres away. The farm's business was bulls; a herd of young Charolais was paddocked on the moor. Much against his better judgement – but despatched by his employer, who had the heart of a vulture – Daniel had braved the fog to check the herd's welfare.

It was a wholly wasted trip as he'd never got that far: his pickup left the road. Which was hardly surprising, he'd sighed: the moors were foul. Near on a miracle he and his dog survived. The pickup was a total wreck. Landed square on its back. Probably sunk into a bog by now.

'Yet you finished up at Gehenna?' said Franklin. 'It was no trouble at all to find us in the fog?'

'Again, sir, that wasn't my choice – I was following Jess's lead. I thought she'd head straight for home, but instead we wound up stumbling onto your property. I would much rather *not* be here, to be honest. It's nothing personal, you understand.'

'I'm sure,' Franklin murmured. 'But now that you *are* here, what did you hope to find?'

'I'd like to use your phone.'

'There is no phone in this house.'

'Then perhaps you'd be so kind as to let me stay here for a while. At least until the fog clears.'

The girls stared at the dour Franklin, who was clearly unamused by the arrival of Daniel. Whether due to his natural peevishness or more specific doubts, he did not appear keen on letting Daniel remain. But on a wretched night like that, who could have been so hard as to turn the young man away? Yet Franklin dithered, and the girls could clearly sense that if it were not for their presence, Daniel would be ejected. Franklin must have exhausted his store of charitable thoughts when he agreed to let the four of *them* stay.

After what seemed an age the old man gave a scowl as deep as a well, and a sigh wheezed out of him, like the coughing of a frog. He glanced down at the dog, which boldly met his gaze. He said, 'Despite my doubts – I'm not happy at all – you may rest here this night. Upon one condition: you cause no nuisance to these girls. I shall allow no you-know-what to take place in my home. And that shotgun of yours must be lodged some place safe, not propped up there by the door. As for that hellhound – '

'She's a deerhound-lurcher, sir.'

'She can be kennelled outside – that is where such creatures should abide.'

They all stared at the dog, which looked uncomfortable. The night was disturbing her too.

A heady atmosphere of tension and excitement gave way to a strained silence. No one seemed certain of what should be done next. Given the lateness of the hour, sleep seemed the safest bet. So the girls went back upstairs, and Daniel was allowed to stay in a room on the ground floor. It was next to Martha's – to stifle any chance of 'hanky-panky things', as Franklin described them. The girls hoped Daniel would be able to sleep. The sound of Martha's snores was like a race between steamrollers ...

* * *

'He's a rather good-looking individual,' said Amy, as the four girls scrambled back into their beds.

Her sister snorted. 'They all look good to you. Even that one from Cheam, who was a total asshole. You spent weeks writing his name over all your school books. Lou's voice then mimicked: 'Oh, Jason – you're divine! Oh, Jason – call me now. Please call me Jason. Call me before I count to a hundred – '

Amy said, 'That's a lie! I never said that once!'

'You *did* – you were moping for weeks.'

At that point Jade chipped in, saying, 'Well Jason sounds an absolute dream, and I don't want to appear a killjoy at his moment but while we're all here sharing our wonderful time, what if we actually are under threat? This new housemate, Daniel – do we believe his tale? Don't you think it's a bit neat, him suddenly turning up like this? It might just be, for the sake of argument, that it was him in the fog when me and Caroline tried to leave. We put the blame on Franklin and thought it was him who made us turn back. But what if we were wrong

– what if it was Daniel? Franklin might have let the biggest freak of all into the house.'

'Oh, thanks a lot, Jade!' said Amy. 'We're supposed to go to sleep now after you've said all that?'

'We should take turns to stay on guard. And you lot should go first, because I'm drained ... '

21

The next morning Caroline was the first to rise. Or so she initially believed. When she padded down to Gehenna's gloomy kitchen - colder than a morgue – she was surprised to find Daniel crouching by the door which led out to the porch. He was feeding titbits to his unhappy dog. She was licking his hand, practically whimpering and wagging an anxious tail.

He said, 'I couldn't sleep – Jess was howling and whining so much I moved out here with her. Air as cold as a vixen's snarl and a lot less sweet. I haven't spent a night like that since Wellbeck got flooded a few years back. Jess fidgeted for hours. The floor's as hard as rock. Blankets are wafer thin.' He stood up, stretching – his tall, lean body stark against the grey fog outside – a statue framed in smoke. 'It's a good job I don't need much. Sleep, that is,' he murmured. 'I'm always up well before dawn.'

Caroline crossed the room towards the massive range; stirred the remaining embers into life. She fed in some twigs and waited until blue flames started to rise. She shoved on a larger log and a pair of peat blocks, watched them spark. She filled up a huge kettle and hung it from the hook which swung above the fire. She said, 'That's my habit: I rise early myself. I generally wake with the dawn, though lately that's been hard. It's difficult to tell if the dawn's arrived – the fog seems to prolong the night. Daytime is one long twilight.'

She started clattering amongst old pots and pans. Trying to come up with one that baked food hadn't spoilt.

She said, 'Things here are fairly rough. And I hope you're keen on meat because we get precious little else apart from a few potatoes. Jade and her veganism had to go right out of the window.'

While strips of meat gently fried – Franklin abhorred them scorched – the pair set out breakfast things, both ever conscious of the towering banks of fog which loomed over the house and flattened out the land. Aware there'd been no change. Aware that, if anything, the gloomy banks were thicker still.

Caroline said, 'Franklin said this fog might last for days.'

'And he could be right,' Daniel murmured. 'This weather's well set in. Needs a good blow of wind. At the moment there's no chance of that.'

'Will you head off home today?'

He said, 'If the old man makes me. To be honest I'd rather stay here - those moors are treacherous at the best of times.'

'We found that out ourselves.'

'Peat and water can be an absolute nightmare ... '

Despite the clattering of pots and pans and the smell of cooking meat, the others still slept on. Caroline pulled a chair up to the weathered oak table. Daniel sat opposite, absorbed by his own thoughts. He fiddled with his thumbs and tension showed round his eyes. He stared at his hands a lot. Caroline was a little wary – Jade's warning was in her mind; but the more she watched Daniel, the more she relaxed. She found it hard to see how he could pose a threat: he did not seem 'the sort'. Which appeared a somewhat reckless way to reach a decision, but people rely on first impressions a great deal. And Caroline's felt good. She sensed no hint of threat. Glimpsed no dishonesty.

She even came to the conclusion that Daniel's self-absorption might be the result of nothing more than a natural shyness. He seemed eager to smile, but held himself in check – needing encouragement. And then she wondered whether this was because of her. Perhaps – living on a farm – he'd not met many girls. *Perhaps* – she blushed at the thought – but it was an intriguing one: perhaps he kind of fancied her ...

Warming to the handsome newcomer all the more, Caroline asked innocently, 'So – do you like it here?'

'In this place?' said Daniel.

'No, the moors. Do you like living on the moors.'

'I guess.' He offered a shrug. 'I've never really known much else. It's kind of a small world but it's OK. My life's been good so far.'

'It must be restricting, though – socially, I should think. It's a long way from any town. Must be hard to make friends. Girls, for instance – you'd not meet many girls.'

'There are girls on the moors, you know – we do have social events! Some of our barn dances are legendary! But yes, I don't meet many of them. You grow up with them all your life, so they're almost like sisters.'

'You've never met a really special one?'

'If I have she passed me by. No one to this point has ever caught my eye.'

Some minutes idled by, then Caroline stood up. 'I'll make us a drink.' She fixed strong coffee, mixed it with powdered milk. They shared the only mug not cracked and rimmed with grease. After a few moments she said, 'Do you know you have a huge weal on your face?'

He said, 'I smacked it on the dash of the pickup.'

She extended one hand. 'And a nasty cut there.' Trembling fingertips hovered above the spot. 'You ought to clean it up.'

'There's a first aid kit?'

She laughed. 'In Gehenna? No telephones or clocks – no mirrors or TV. What do you think – they have a first aid kit? I'll try and fix it, if you like – '

'If I'm putting my safety in your hands, I ought to at least know your name.'

She said, 'I'm Caroline. Caroline Marchant.'

While Caroline tended to his wound, Daniel began to talk about the house they now both shared. He said, 'Do you know this place is steeped in tales?'

She said, 'I didn't know, but I'm hardly surprised. It seems the kind of place that makes you wonder if there are real bogeymen.'

Daniel said, 'In years past, folk called it the 'House of Death'. We used to get threatened with it if we were naughty when we were kids. Our parents would say, 'If you're not careful we'll take you across the moors and leave you at the door of Gehenna.' For almost eighteen years I've lived around these parts and this is the only time I've ventured this close. I used to think the folk who lived here must be like things out of Hell.'

Caroline used a dampened strip torn from Daniel's check shirt to clean dirt from the wound. 'Do you think Franklin's from Hell?'

'He's certainly weird enough. You wouldn't mistake him for a local primary school teacher. What do you make of him?'

Caroline shrugged. 'He's definitely odd. And his sister's odd as well. But there isn't a law against that.'

'Maybe not. But some of those tales – the ones that go way back – there must be something in there. These legends don't come out of nowhere … '

They broke off as a movement in the hall preceded the entrance of a bleary-eyed Amy. She walked in yawning, stretching, scratching her head. 'Is this a private do or can anyone join in?' She had her sleeping bag wrapped round her like a shawl. Its trailing edge was dragging on the floor.

'Anyone made any coffee?'

'There's hot water on the stove.'

'A decent friend would get up and make me a cup.'

Amy slumped down on a chair. Cradled her head on her arms. She said, 'I take it the nightmare's still real … '

22

Gradually the kitchen filled up as others wandered in – all of them crotchety, cold and half-asleep.

First in was Franklin, offering not a word. Next in was his sister, greasy hair tied up, her flat feet bare. Then came Jade – intense and pale – enigmatically grave – warily watching them all. Lastly, Lou stumbled in, befuddled by the hour: always slow to wake up, struggling to find words. She croaked, 'What time is it?' and everybody shrugged. None of them had a clue.

'So then,' Franklin murmured, finding the will at last to break a long silence. 'All here for breakfast – a rather gloomy bunch. All due to that mad beast which howled for half the night. If you can't control that animal you will have to secure it in one of the barns. While you are here, boy,' – his gaze fixed on Daniel – 'you will please obey my rules, and not disrupt our sleep. And it would be fair and reasonable, would it not, if while you are here you offered to provide some work to help pay for your maintenance? Do I make myself clear?'

Daniel said, 'Perfectly – I have no problem with that. I'm grateful to you, sir, for being such a generous host.'

'Ha! I'll have no backchat. No sarcasm or 'wit'.'

'No, sir. I can see that.'

With his rules firmly laid down, Franklin mellowed enough to wolf a plate of food. Breakfast was a tense affair, though, nobody spoke much. There was much jostling of elbows and exchanges of sour looks. Seven people were huddled around a table built for four, and none could eat in peace. Apart from Martha – who seemed to find great delight in the press of bodies and restive flesh. It caused her to giggle uncontrollably. In the brief moments when her giggling subsided, she leaned close to sniff at those around her.

Ignoring the antics of his sister, Franklin licked his knife clean and dropped it on his plate. He spoke to Daniel: 'You can help me down below. I am excavating there – reinforcing old crossbeams. I'm trying to open up some new rooms in the rock.'

'Is there a need for that?'

Franklin looked dumbstruck. 'A need?' he sputtered out. 'Was there a need for me to take you in last night? Do I have any 'need' to watch your idiotic face sneering at what I do? It's not a question of what you might deem wise – rather it is a matter of what your hosts desire!'

'I didn't mean to imply – ' Daniel paused and gave a shrug. Some things aren't worth the time …

As the pair walked from the room, Caroline offered Daniel a wry and friendly smile. For a lingering moment their glances met and locked. It seemed that much was said without a single word. Then Daniel turned away, spurred by a dog-like growl from the moody Franklin.

'I'll see you later,' he said, as he walked out.

Amy caught Caroline's eye and stuck up both her thumbs.

'I think he fancies you.'

'Don't be ridiculous!'

But Caroline looked pleased.

23

It all formed a potent mix: the arrival of Daniel and the tensions of the girls. Having been for so long stifled by the claustrophobic atmosphere of Gehenna, the girls embraced the change as though they'd been given freshly oxygenated air. Their demeanour transformed: their hearts were lightened simply through having him around. It got to the stage where emotions set to work. Hormones began to stir. A certain sexual chemistry filled the air. Good-natured rivalry became the order of the day as each of them tried her best to be the one to shine out, to be radiant amidst their squalid surroundings.

It was the sharp minded Amy who was the first to emphasize what quickly became clear to all of them: Daniel only had eyes for Caroline. Of course Amy blamed this on Caroline's head start. 'She got up at the crack of dawn to make sure she got in first! The rest of us never stood a chance. And not only that,' she said, 'but she bandaged up his wounds!'

'I didn't bandage them – I just wiped off some dirt.'

'Ha! And we all know the significance of that. I read that novel *A Farewell to Arms* – the poor patient and the nurse – that Hemingway dude knew what he was up to. The next thing we know you'll be snogging him!'

'Don't be ridiculous!' Caroline said.

'I would,' said Amy. 'I'd snog him right off his feet. If he gets hurt again it's going to be me who gets in first with the love and attention and bandages.'

But it was the more serious Lou who was the most smitten: Lou, who had always been boy-clumsy, boy-shy, and naïve in the matter of relationships. She was wholly unprepared for the impact Daniel had on her emotions. Unable to relax. Unable even to sit down in case he found reason to walk from the room.

She needed always to be there, to be near him, to hear his voice. She became addicted to the surges of passion in her veins: a passion so intense it made the world rotate faster on its axis. She spent so much time fancying him it gave her a headache.

As that first day progressed her infatuation grew – until it was impossible to miss. The others ribbed her about it: humorously at first, but as the day wore on the humour wore off. The jokes became barbs snagging the skin of her innocence. It wasn't her fault that she'd never been on a date. It wasn't her doing that she'd never been kissed. In the grotesque world of Gehenna with all its tensions, fears, suspicions and pressures, these things gained an additional significance.

The more she tried to laugh away the jokes the more they stung inside.

She was learning about jealousy: a lovelorn kind of jealousy. And the knowledge that she had been overlooked.

* * *

Lou could not sleep that night for the tingling in her blood and the pounding in her chest. One floor away from her was the cause of her desire. So unbearably close – so distant in his thoughts. No amount of yearning could tear his besotted gaze from her good friend Caroline. It seemed so utterly unfair that Lou could never once catch anybody's eye – ignite a fire of passion in another person's heart. Tossing and turning helped to a degree, but only for the few brief moments such movements could occupy.

Finally Lou got up: she was going to toss and turn all night if she didn't do something.

She padded downstairs, planning to make a drink. Not because she was thirsty, simply to block her thoughts.

The kind of thoughts that could drive her mad: turning, turning, turning again. Aimlessly, inside a void.

24

Surrounded by the night, Lou sat in the cold embrace of Gehenna's dark kitchen. The world was silent, as if all life had ceased. The air of Gehenna was funereally still. Nothing: no creaking boards – no sleepy night-time coughs – no curtain-stirring draughts. The range fire had subsided to a pile of greyish ash and there was not enough heat to bring water to the boil.

Instead of hot coffee Lou sipped a tooth-tingling measure of gritty well-water.

She wandered restively from the chilly kitchen, trying to shake off her mood.

Followed the lengthy main hallway – sinister, still and cold. Past the dark dining room – deserted, no one home. Around the sudden bend which granted access to the remaining ground-floor rooms.

As Lou continued forward, her tired thoughts rambling, she thought she heard a creak, like floorboards up ahead.

Perhaps Franklin was still awake – busy in the library.

Curiosity led her on.

But the library was empty. Nothing had disturbed the air. The dust lay undisturbed.

As she was about to wander back, Lou paused – squinted and stared.

The barest gleam of light showed around the frame of the inner door.

The door to the study.

Maybe Franklin was in there, doing some paperwork.

'Franklin?'

Heard no reply. Tapped softly on the door. No answer – all alone.

Study door not locked, eased it open a touch. Emboldened, she pushed some more and followed it into the room.

A smell of paper and dust.

The reek of Franklin's clothes.

Crunching dirt underfoot.

The source of the meagre light was an old paraffin lamp, standing on top of a desk. It had been turned off, but was not quite extinguished. A feeble ring of flame showed around the short, charred wick. Easy to overlook – turn it down and walk away. Happens almost every day.

Lou had gone this far, so why grow cautious now? She grasped the small brass knob which raised and lowered the wick. Moved it a quarter-turn.

The flame faltered, then strengthened.

Burned with a yellow hue.

The ancient rosewood desk appeared practically crushed by the items heaped upon it.

A mass of paper: perhaps a thousand sheets. A tall, teetering pile of scribbles and designs. Ink pots, pencils and pens. Blotters, rulers and pins. Stapler and paper punch.

And fresher pages – dense writing – neatly stacked.

Tempting to take a look – read through the first few lines.

And then read on some more.

Turn the first page over.

Sit down – adjust the light …

25

Five hundred years ago. How different was a life? Lou was discovering.

What she had started reading was part of a massive book begun decades before by Franklin's ancestors. A work of tale and truth: a record and a view of how things might have been. Each generation had added its own thoughts, had re-written and revised much of what went before. A constant reappraisal wrought by obsessive research, guesswork and hope. The oldest memories had almost faded out, but that was no hindrance to future, fertile minds, which simply made things up or adapted what they'd found to fit in with their times.

Part epic fantasy, part documented fact – what Lou was perusing was a perverse work of art. She was not sure if it was meant to be believed or had been devised to entertain.

But Franklin had played his part, had joined the obsessed ranks of those who'd toiled before. How many quiet nights must he have spent searching through the ancient family files, tracking down long-lost books? How many jars of ink had he drained in order to compile it? How many pencil stubs had wound up on the floor? How many smudged and spoiled sheets of paper had he torn up? How many painful hours had he spent easing out the cramps from his writing hand?

The first page was a terse summary of the historical base:

> In the sixteenth century the English King, Henry VIII, severed ties with the established Church of Rome. Religion in England was split into factions. The followers of Rome were hunted and despised. Their monasteries were sacked, their wealth spirited away and their clergy hounded out.
>
> The entire kingdom was riven by hatred, and a cancerous distrust forced whole families apart. Cruel soldiers were despatched to track fugitive priests. Some soldiers reached the moor.

So terse was the passage that Lou concluded that the facts must be well-documented elsewhere. What most concerned Franklin in the tale which he set down were the effects on Gehenna – an uncommonly grand house of the time. Owned by the Lord Cornwell, a fine God-fearing man. Though not one Franklin admired.

In fact, Lou quickly came to realize that Franklin's views were completely biased, and that he must have used creative thought to flesh out much of what was known. For no one could truly quote discourses from the past, nor so bring the dead to life:

'You are Sir John Cornwell – the Master of this house – upholder of the faith?'

'I am,' said Cornwell.

'That faith which stems from Rome? That faith which grants to the Pope powers in excess of the powers of our King?'

'I am a Christian,' Cornwell said. 'The Pope and kings aside, I claim God as my judge.'

The sergeant grunted as he slid down from his horse, landing before his troop on a mud which swamped his shins. He said, 'Let's go inside – '

'As you wish,' Lord Cornwell said, stepping back from his porch.

The soldier, Thomas Gaunt, gazed on a high-roofed room decked with the trappings of wealth. He said, 'It seems a fruitful position – straddling a major trading route from the farms to the east coast ports. My humble soldier's pay would not stretch towards this. Fine glasses brought from France. Tapestries on the walls – '

'As you hint – trade does pay.'

'Quite so,' Gaunt murmured, as he raised a pewter mug. He weighed it in his hands and marvelled at its feel. Then he said: 'And all your wealth – spiritual and earthly – must make you well content.'

He put the heavy jug down and scraped some of the mud from his boots, He sat down on a bench, placing his sword on the floor. He said: 'But you're cut off out here, your home's remote – '

'The traders bring me news.'

'So you'll well know, then, that King Henry himself has broken ties with Rome, and denounced all papal rights. And that, while we converse, monasteries are being purged across the length and breadth of this entire realm?'

'Of course,' said Cornwell, reclining in his chair – tugging free his rich gown which had snagged on the rough floor. 'None but the blind and deaf could fail to know the crimes committed in God's name.'

'Ah – 'tis a crime then to honour your true King – rightful head of the Church – defender of God's Law?'

'If our King commits no crime, the same cannot be said of those whom he employs … '

As was their legal right, the band of soldiers searched the house from roof to floor. They searched the larders and bedrooms, the great hall. They lifted every screen and arras from the walls. They looked for secret rooms – holes hidden behind boards. They rammed iron spikes through the floors.

While they were searching they 'interviewed' the staff: those employed in the house, and those who worked the fields. Each one declared their faith; each one said that they knew nothing of priests or monks.

'Ah, 'tis a waste of time,' Gaunt said, as he glanced around a muddy, fog-cloaked yard. 'Another goose chase, another wasted ride. Yet one more fruitless probe into other people's lives.'

'I'd swear there are monks here, though,' said one of his brigade. 'I know them by their smell. It seldom fails me – my instinct is renowned. But who knows where they're hid - we've torn this house apart.'

'Perhaps they're in the roof?' said another.

'That's been checked,' said Gaunt. 'We've checked it all.'

'Out in the fields then – disguised in shepherds' rags?'

'Mayhap,' the sergeant sighed, 'but we can't pick 'em out. Methinks we'll head back home; try to make Chesterfield before darkness descends.'

'Inside this fog, Tom?' said a soldier. 'We'll be blessed! Marshes are such death traps on the finest of days!'

'Aye, it may be you are right. It would do no harm for us to rest here. Commandeer one of the more comfortable barns. Send someone to the kitchen for food.'

26

In one of the many massive barns erected around the house, the soldiers settled down. They tethered their horses beside them, saw them fed. They wrapped themselves in cloth and burrowed into the straw. They cursed as beads of fog dripped from the beams above, swore as their horses dreamed …

'I swear, Tom, this day swerved so much from sun to mist that it seems barely natural.'

'Do you know your trouble, Dick?' Gaunt said, as he gave vent to an enormous expression of flatulence, 'you have a suspicious mind. Every natural thing makes you itch. The rising of the sun, the falling of the moon – all those things trouble you. There ain't no witches out there creating fog. There ain't no shades or ghosts prowling in graveyard rags. That fog comes from the ground: 'tis naught but the steaming breath of the world.'

'You don't know everything.'

'Aye now, that's true, Dick, I don't know much at all. Yet I do know that I am both hungry and wet. I know that I need some rest, or I shall get depressed.'

Dick said, 'This fog be the Devil's work.'

Gaunt dozed for half an hour – until a black rat on his chest made him snap wide awake.

He jumped up, cursing, bemused by where he was. Went lumbering in the dark, woke up a nervy horse. Crashed hard into a beam and lurched backwards with a moan. 'God's truth I hate this work. Are you awake there?' Nobody answered him. His soldiers were asleep: their snores near raised the roof.

Angered at being ignored, the sergeant grabbed his cloak, and stumbled from the barn.

'My name is Robert Jilkes,' a voice hissed close at hand, making Gaunt emit a cry.

'Hell's teeth – blasted fool! What kind of jape is this? If you'd fain stop my heart you've made a powerful start!'

'A thousand pardons, sir – I thought you saw me here.'

'Oh, my eyes split the dark, do they? What be you doing, man, grovelling in this fog?'

'Waiting upon you, sir – hoping to crave a word.'

''Bout what?'

'About three priests who shelter in this house. I have heard of a reward … '

At the following break of day Gaunt gathered his bedraggled men together, and said, 'Three priests are sheltering. We have an informer who I believe speaks true. He serves God and the King – and his own empty pockets. Of the first two I might doubt, but I'd challenge any man to turn his back on gold. I require this place to be surrounded while I talk with Lord Cornwell – I'll give him the benefit of having misunderstood. Offer the Lord a final chance to prove he serves the King. Else we'll take him as well … '

'Lord Cornwell, last afternoon I asked you to your face if you had harboured priests. You plain denied this – '

'As I shall do again.'

'And will you, too, deny that your cellar has false walls? And will you swear to my face that, couched behind those walls, is not a cabal of quaking priests?'

'I – '

'You shield three heretics who, far from lauding God, praise the Pontiff of Rome in all his corrupt works! Men who abandoned prayer so they could garner gold with which to dress their Pope!'

'Such men are Christians!'

'Aye, aren't we all, Sir John? But Christians come and go – while some fall at waysides. 'Tis not my place to judge; I merely serve the King. This hunt be the King's will.'

And thus it was that with little to be done the Lord Cornwell reluctantly yielded up the three priests. The estate staff gathered as silent witnesses as Gaunt mounted his horse; saw the doomed priests tied with ropes. He gazed back at the house to meet John Cornwell's gaze with a fierce one of his own. If he felt pleasure, he kept it to himself. If he bristled with pride it was not revealed. He simply spurred his horse away, leaving Cornwell wondering if he would come for him next …

27

Lou rubbed her bloodshot eyes as the hissing lantern's fumes stabbed at them, made them sting. She was growing sleepy, yet wanted to read more: her chance might disappear if she relinquished it now. Franklin might not be keen on letting strangers share in his mysterious tale.

Was what she did illegal? Probably not, she guessed. Did it smack of deceit? Most certainly, she thought. But it was worth some guilt – Lou had always adored delving in history ...

> Robert Jilkes, who had served his King by revealing the three false priests was of our family. Naturally he was soon found out, and called to give account before his lord – obligated to justify his loyalty to the Crown. Pilloried for his belief in the one true God above, and his scorn of the Pope.
>
> Which was the greatest act of perfidy performed by that self-serving knave and traitor, John Cornwell. For it was the Lord Cornwell who sinned against his God and gainsaid his own King.
>
> Prompted no doubt by shame, and the burden of his guilt, Cornwell craved a vile revenge. He had our ancestor stripped bare, mocked, tortured, fouled and scourged. Had him carried broken, in chains, to the building's core. Had him condemned to prowl, sightless, hungry and sore, in darkness without end.
>
> Caged like an unloved beast in the cellar of the house, our ancestor wailed. He begged a pittance of mercy and screamed out a thousand oaths. He beseeched to be released and craved solace from his foes. Flung himself at the door, ripped lumps from the earth walls with fingers turned to claws. But no one could save him; none would grant relief from the insects and rats which viewed him as their feast. No one would stem the tide of pain that hopped and crawled from cracks in the floor.
>
> Alone inside his infernal prison, Robert felt the days and weeks extend into long months. No mercy would come from the wrath of Lord Cornwell. Nor would death come quickly, sparing him his fate. He would know endless years of pain and suffering: disease, hunger and loneliness.
>
> His only contact with the world beyond the door was

through the estate's new maid, who brought his daily food. Food unfit for a dog. Food spat upon and soured. Food that was cursed by Cornwell's spite.

'Agnes,' he said one day as the shy young maid appeared, 'what kind of looks have you?'

The girl's cheeks reddened, and she faltered in the act of sliding a plate of food towards Robert's waiting hands. Her long fingers touched her hair and, quite unconsciously, she rearranged her locks.

She said, 'They're not much,' though she was too modest. Agnes had held the eye of every man she met. Even the Lord Cornwell had seen fit to admire her flourishing good looks.

'What colour hair have you?'

'An autumn shade of brown. Long curls conceal my eyes.'

'Which are?'

Agnes glanced round. Saw she was unobserved - (she had been expressly forbidden to have any form of discourse with Robert). She quickly knelt down on the earth, the better to slip her words through the small feeding space at the base of the door. She said, 'My eyes are brown and flecked by a shade of green not common in these parts.'

'And have you family?'

'Most of them died last year. Stricken down by fever from bad water in the well.'

'Mine have died too, Agnes. And how I envy them for escaping my fate.'

'You should not say that – '

'But why – what life have I? Animals in the fields at least gaze on the sky. All I can see is gloom. Gloom between prison walls. Gloom rising from my heart.'

Agnes became his only friend. Her youthful innocence wept for his wicked plight. Lonely herself, and made fearful by the lust of men on the estate, she leaned towards the comfort of Robert Jilkes - the only man who had never threatened her. The only one who cared ...

'Robert, I have brought your food.'

The luckless Robert stirred in the grim cellar's heart. 'Maggoty fat again?' he said.

'Not this time,' Agnes breathed. 'I've stolen shanks of lamb, Also some still-fresh beef. The dogs have fought for it, but there is bone to suck. Still marrow left inside.'

She held the food out, as Robert slowly crawled across the filthy floor – his limbs crippled and sore. On such a meagre diet his bones were turning soft and his muscles were grown thin. As was his breathing, now just a laboured rasp. He had to shred his food, for his teeth had rotted out. But though Agnes shook with dread, still brave Robert hung on. His heart and will would not die.

28

'How long has it been now? Robert asked one fateful day when anguish gripped his soul. 'Has a year passed yet?'

Agnes said, 'Almost two. Another autumn comes – the fields wear yellow cowls. Last night the year's first frost laid flat the unmown corn and drove the geese off their eggs. The Master flogged us, as though the fault was ours.'

'I cannot tell,' Robert said, with a voice so weak she could barely hear his words. 'In here 'tis always cold. The summer comes and goes but the air remains the same. I am so lonely!' he cried, with tears of grief. 'I have not seen the sky since fate had me condemned. Nor seen a human face, nor enjoyed any human touch. Not felt a warming hand.' He gave a huge sob. 'And now my memory fades. Even Lord Cornwell's face is vanished from my mind. No one remembers me … '

'That is not true Robert: Agnes never forgets you. Who is it feeds you and prays that you'll be well?'

'That's true,' he said softly, as he regained himself. 'And that's my worst regret: that my gaze never once has lingered on your face. How cruel my life is that I am denied even the image of the green flecks in your eyes. If I had just touched your hand – '

Agnes lay at full stretch, saying, 'Touch my hand now…'

And thus the pair embarked upon a sad affair they knew would end in pain. What kind of future could thwarted lovers have – kept apart by a lord whose home formed prison walls? How could they ever know the blessed peace on earth once promised to all men? For they were the unfortunate victims of Lord Cornwell's endless shame: a shame he was never able to ease despite the flow of years. All they could do was dream and caress with fingertips. Make plans destined to fail.

But the situation changed when Cornwell caught Agnes in conversation with Robert. With a roar of anger, he snatched her in his arms. Carried her struggling through the yard to the main hall. In the floor there was a trapdoor through which he, at times, had peered down on Robert. Enraged, he raised it to bellow into the gloom. Cried out: 'Here comes the wench

you have strained so hard to lure!' He cast her through
the trap with a malicious laugh. Then bolted it once more ...
Darkness ruled

the tale went on

> a darkness so complete it seemed fashioned for tombs. Far more imprisoning, it was, than earth and stone. Its strain on sanity almost too great to bear. In darkness few things move, few live, and those which do are belly-bound and foul. And the pair were hungry, for no one brought them food. They had to lick moisture from puddles on the floor. In time they learned to kill black rats, and drink their blood. Else they'd have not survived ...
>
> 'Eat, Agnes,' Robert urged. 'You must keep up your strength.'
>
> 'No more,' Agnes pleaded. 'I'll chew no more flesh from worms and creeping bugs. I'll gnaw no more dead rats to nourish on their blood.'
>
> 'No – you must stay alive, for while we are alive there always will be hope. All is not over – we can survive down here. Already I've begun to excavate our world. I have hewn out a room adjacent to this. Come, Agnes - come and see.'
>
> But Agnes protested. 'What happiness can come from living like the rats: despised, ignored and scorned?
>
> 'The rats will be our friends. Though men have cast us out – this world may take us in ... '
>
> A strange beauty

Lou read

> was evinced by the gallant pair's desperate struggles for life. They hacked out tunnels, clawed them with tooth and nail. They fashioned walls and rooms – passageways – gaping halls. They made friends with the darkness and found their strength coming back as effort gained reward. As they toiled like demons inside that choking gloom, they found cold, gushing streams and flint fragments fit for tools. And, though

their eyesight slowly failed, they learned to move about by means of sound and touch.

One day our forefather said: 'Hark to those howls above! What new torment is this?'

The pair put down their well-used tools, the better to devote their attention to shrill cries of distress from overhead. Cries filled with grief and blame, anguish, torment and shame, and references to *Plague!*

While the couple had eked out an existence down below, the household up above had been struck by Black Death: that terrible disease which, like divine rebuke, had gobbled half of Europe. Lord Cornwell's family and staff were black with boils: rot dribbled from their wounds and cramps racked their legs and arms. The punishment he had feared – in a manner unforeseen – had laid claim to John Cornwell. That was an awful time, as screams rang through the night and wailing filled the days. Above, huge bonfires were lit to purge the air. The victims were hounded out – sealed up or burned alive. Yet nothing stopped the Plague – nothing held back that tide of loss and destruction.

Only our shocked kin – who seemed immune to plague – escaped the dreadful swish of Death's harvesting blade. While others fell like corn they, the pawns of fickle fate, survived to tell the tale. They, with their ironic diet of festering rat flesh. They with their draughts of blood, and supplementing bugs. It seemed almost as though they had been overlooked by Death. Or, for some unknown reason, spared …

'Agnes, 'tis silent now, the household must have fled. Or else all souls lie dead. We can escape now.'

'To what?' Agnes replied. 'To a land of pestilence with no safe place to hide? No, Robert – we are secure down here, we have survived – let us not grow reckless now. We should keep building this home that we have conceived. Turn our backs to the light - shun perils and disease. God rejected His world and let its people die. Let us seek gods down here.'

And so the pair eschewed the realm of mortal kind in favour of their world. They continued building, extending their strange home. While mortals died above, they prospered in the dark. They thought they must be blessed, that someone down below was looking out for them.

And in time fair Agnes gave birth to a strong and healthy son. The pair gave him a name – though that has since been lost.

No one ever described the family's final fate – for no one ever witnessed it …

29

Lou put the pages down: though she was still absorbed, her tired eyes had read enough.

She leaned back, stretching the joints along her spine; she had been hunching forward, as if glued to the desk. Weary hands smoothed her hair – rubbed elbows – wrapped themselves around cold upper arms.

So cold had the night become that she could watch her breath stream out across the study like a ghost who was running late.

So still was Gehenna, even the sound of the flames in the lamp could be heard.

Lou tiptoed from the room. She would have to find a chance to read more later on. The ornate walls watched her as she padded along the main hall. The carvings on the stairs stood more lifelike than before. While mortal beings slept, Gehenna came alive in some mysterious way.

But if Lou noticed this, she kept it to herself – best not to interfere with things which can't exist. The world is full of science, Lou knew this for a fact. All else could be shrugged off.

At the base of the looming stairs – just at the point of beginning to ascend – Lou was brought to a halt.

A distant, low noise thrummed through the cold still air. A tiny bead of light showed round the cellar door. Could someone be inside at that hour of the night – was Franklin padding around?

Though she was weary, Lou was also intrigued.

On elfin soft footsteps she crept towards the door.

She eased the stiff wood back a fraction and peered inside.

Oil lanterns had been lit …

* * *

Wholly committed now to her curiosity, Lou risked the cellar's murk. Smoky light guided her, but in erratic bursts. Long tracts of Stygian bloom crowded between each flame. Silence lay all around. It lurked furtively ahead. It prowled stealthily behind.

Lou started breathing with short and ragged gasps. As if the corpse-cold air sucked the warmth from her lungs –

Or maybe it was just the tension growing inside making her chest contract.

A thud followed a dull thud. The pounding of Lou's heart roared loud inside the gloom.

She glanced behind her – she could still see the door.

She took a few more steps then the path she followed veered.

She looked behind again.

All that she could see now were a few dwindling lights.

The cellar walls closed in, and Lou found herself walking the labyrinth proper.

She saw no hint of Franklin, although she glimpsed the signs of his tunnelling work: new pit props, scattered tools, side tunnels abandoned, as if he'd vainly searched for treasure in the walls.

Why dig new tunnels, though, when there already were literally kilometres of them arrowing through the earth?

Fresh ones at every turn, burrowing out of sight like the strands of some great black web.

As Lou advanced further, the tunnels began to take on a more ordered aspect. They were more skilful than the shafts already walked – more artful in design – 'cultured', almost. The early passageways were clumsy, rough affairs; these latter, more refined.

It began to dawn on Lou that she was walking through the primeval, eerie realm of Agnes and Robert Jilkes.

The more the pair had toiled, the better they'd become. Their craft had vastly improved.

And still she padded on, though she had by this time become hopelessly lost.

So many offshoots and bifurcations came: so many twists and turns and unexpected curves. A bloodhound would have strained to find its way back home. Would just have sat and howled.

Yet Lou was drawn ahead – partly because she felt so tired that she almost believed she'd passed into a dream.

Partly she was enthralled, for the dreadful, stark beauty gave her a sense of awe …

30

At last the labyrinth unveiled its fearsome pinnacle: the rooms where the doomed couple had lived.

Dungeon-like chambers appeared before Lou's eyes – great, cavernous affairs whose domes loomed like night skies. Cells in which meals had been served, tools fashioned, plans prepared. One where Agnes had given birth.

And there were huge blocks – like altars, or perhaps the slabs where butchers toil – channelled as if for blood.

And, underneath the blocks, stone basins chiselled out as if to catch the stuff.

The subterranean world became even more sinister as new rooms were revealed.

Inside a long tract of darkness where the lamps had either been removed or had consumed all their fuel, Lou stumbled on some cells in which there still remained signs of activity.

The faintest glimmer from a lamp some distance off was sufficient to expose bloodstains upon the floors.

And small splinters of bone, where creatures had been gnawed. And ominously large chains …

Lou had to clench her teeth in order to prevent herself from vomiting. Such an obscene stench was hanging in the air. The stench of dirt and graves – of gangrene and decay. A stench of such vigour that Lou could not convince herself it came from far-off days.

No, this was too rich, too potent to ascribe to some festering corpse which had fallen years before. It had a fresh bouquet, despite its putrid edge. Its source was in the here and now.

Lou began to back away. She had seen far too much: she had to leave that place. She started sprinting back through the rooms and shafts – glad to find renewed strength in her legs, heart and lungs. Strength bolstered by the fear that if she paused to think, everything might be lost.

Lou could not say why she had such an awful sense that something had emerged from its underground lair. But in a few short moments her worst fears were confirmed. For the thing from the tunnels came after her …

31

Darkness advanced behind, for each lantern guttered and died as Lou's pursuer passed. So great was its pace that it seemed as though a tide of massive, silent waves was powering through the shafts. Swallowing all it touched, obliterating sight and dampening every sound. In fact, the few sounds which could be heard emerged from Lou's own body: her steps, her breaths, her words.

The words merged into one. One long and dreadful scream. One desperate cry for help.

How hard Lou battled, though, to flee that labyrinth and leave her fate behind. Despite the panic which was coursing through her veins; despite the terrible fear which wreaked havoc in her brain; still her lungs pumped away, like the pistons of a battleship. Taking her through chambers in which the dead appeared to have returned to life as long shadows on the floors. Taking her down narrow shafts where bloodstains on the walls were transferred to her sleeves.

And yet the hunter gained, for its awful, silent tide proved irresistible.

It pressed so close behind at times that Lou could feel its spray; the spittle from its lips went spurting past her face –

Sometimes so near that she could breathe it in.

Nothing like a black tide at all.

But a thing of time-wrecked flesh …

In the end Lou realized that she would have to make a stand: one cannot outrun death for ever. She searched for something in the tunnels fit to use against her imminent foe, and snatched up one of Franklin's tools. A pickaxe so heavy that when she grabbed it she was swung clean her off her feet.

She scrambled up, panting hard, clutching the haft of the axe so tightly that droplets of blood were squeezed from her hands. She squinted at the darkness from which death would come and tried to calm her ravaged thoughts.

And Lou's unseen hunter paused. Perhaps it felt unsure. Or perhaps it savoured this. Perhaps it relished the desperate fight for life which Lou was pledged to start, entirely concealed from the sight of the world. Unaided and alone – trembling and yet strangely calm – clueless as to what she faced.

For an age it lingered – threatening in the dark. Then its snarling face appeared and terror gripped Lou's heart. She raised her weapon high, but before she could strike out, cold fingers closed around her throat …

32

In the morning Amy awoke to a soft, grey, moody light and said, 'Lou, you still asleep?' She received no answer from the far end of the room where Lou's narrow bed stood, indistinct and still in gloom. She sat up in bed, rubbed her eyes, looked around. 'Anybody know what the weather is like?'

'Still foggy,' said Jade, who was buried in a cocoon of bedding. 'I had a look out earlier.'

Amy crept from her bed. She went to a window and rubbed her fingertips across a pane covered in condensation. Said, 'It's even worse than before – it's like a smoke machine out there.' She dived back into bed, then once more glanced down the room. Finally saw that Lou's bed was empty.

'Do you know where Lou is?'

Jade shrugged, under her sheets.

'Her bed's not been slept in.'

'Perhaps she stayed downstairs. Maybe she couldn't sleep for thinking of Daniel, and went to be near him.'

'Don't be ridiculous ... ' But no simple answer seemed to account for Lou's chilly and unused bed. Amy said, 'I'll go look.'

'Before you go,' said Jade, 'bank up that fire a bit.'

Trembling from the cold, Amy dressed with haste, threw logs onto the fire then trotted off down the stairs. She tried a few rooms, but each appeared empty. The whole of Gehenna was deserted and still. It echoed in the way abandoned warehouses do when birds fly through them.

Only in the kitchen did Amy find some life: Franklin stood by a bench, hacking up chunks of meat.

'Are you ready for breakfast?'

'Not yet,' Amy replied. 'I'm looking for someone.'

But searching high and low only succeeded in confirming Lou's absence. Not only was Amy's sister missing, but all her bags had gone. Some time during the night all her things had vanished. Every memory and trace – down to a screwed tissue – had simply disappeared.

Feeling increasingly uneasy Amy returned downstairs, where she found Franklin still engaged in preparing some food.

He said, 'Have you found her yet, whoever you have lost?'

'No,' Amy said, sighing. 'I've been looking for my sister.'

'The plump one?'

'She's not plump,' Amy said. 'Just about the wrong side of thin. You haven't seen her, have you?'

The old man shrugged. He appeared to search his thoughts while filleting a joint of meat. But found nothing of worth until he had a row of fillets sizzling in a pan.

'Not since last evening,' he lied, wiping his hands, 'when I came across her in the hallway, where she was angry and tearful. It transpired she had been teased, and was debating whether she should strike out alone.'

Amy was shell-shocked. 'Do you mean she's left the house?'

'I never saw her leave,' said Franklin. 'But she may have done. I tried to dissuade her, but who knows what she did after I retired to my bed?'

33

Amy roused her two friends, and with the assistance of Daniel the house was searched again. Amy just could not believe that Lou would had gone without saying goodbye or without leaving any signs. They'd had their ups and downs – as any sisters do – but they'd never split up. Amy kept saying this: 'Lou would never walk away. She'd not get that upset; she'd not leave me behind.'

'So where is she?' Daniel said.

'I wish I knew, Daniel. Maybe out in the grounds – '

Daniel volunteered to search, with the aid of his lurcher, Jess. The girls stayed in the porch. Not through nervousness, but because Amy felt, as if by a sixth sense, that Lou was still near the house. Possibly right inside. Possibly hidden away. Maybe playing a perverse, unfunny game.

'Of course, the other thing it might be,' Amy said, 'is that Lou's simply lost. This is a huge house, with more rooms than we can count. It's also pretty old, so might have secret space. Priest holes and passageways, concealed cupboards and doors – who knows what it contains? Just take that labyrinth – that place could stretch for kilometres ... '

'But Franklin's checked down there,' said Jade.

'That's what he says. I wouldn't trust that man to give me the right time of day.'

The girls stirred anxiously as Daniel's outline loomed, sinister in the murk. 'I can't find her out here,' he called, as he approached. 'But it's so thick with fog a whole army could disappear. I've searched through some outbuildings, and over by the gate, and checked out as far as the swamp.'

'What about footprints?' said Amy.

Daniel laughed. 'I'm a farmhand, Amy, not a professional tracker.' He bent to tether Jess. The dog shook fog droplets off, as though they made her itch.

The four went back into the house and sat, as if at a particularly mournful wake, around the kitchen table.

'I can still *feel* her,' said Amy, 'that's what's strange. As if Lou hasn't gone but is still close at hand. Something is in the air, a vibration or scent: a 'presence' of some kind.'

Daniel looked sceptical, but a grave Jade sympathized. She said, 'It has been proved that some people can feel such things. I guess with relatives you would sense it all the more, because you have such powerful bonds.'

'That's right,' said Amy. 'One time, when I was ill, even before I knew, Lou said, 'Something's wrong'. She could pick up on it, in the same way that you hear of twins sharing each other's pain.'

Jade said, 'Perhaps, too, if you feel things this strongly, you ought to keep looking until someone proves you wrong. If Lou's in need of help, it might be her strength of will that's calling out to you.'

'I can't believe that!' said Daniel.

Amy shrugged. 'All I can say for sure is that I feel Lou near. Almost inside this room, almost here in my hands – '

Behind her, a huge stew-pan boiled.

* * *

Amy was so encouraged by Jade's enthusiastic support that she felt moved to search the house for a third time. Jade, in fact, accompanied her, for she was so convinced by Amy's great belief that she shared in it herself. She had it in her mind that Amy would be drawn to Lou, like a moth to a flame. For months Jade had wondered about strange, unproven powers: about telepathy, mind-melding, 'spirit' acts , the 'beyond'.

She felt she might be close to witnessing such things.

But, oh, how wrong Jade was …

* * *

'What do you think?' Daniel asked, when he and Caroline found themselves alone in the cold kitchen. 'Is Lou in hiding?'

'I doubt deliberately. If it started as a joke it would have palled by now. I'm afraid I'm rather of the view that Lou's 'presence' has left. It is just we three … '

'Plus me.'

'Plus you, of course.' Caroline produced a smile – the first one for some time. So much had been going wrong that the girls were running out of looks other than frowns. She continued teasingly, 'Of course, I don't even know you – '

'That's my cue to begin?'

'With what?'

'With who I am. With the things that make me tick – '

The smile remained on Caroline's face. Where it glowed like a low, warm flame …

34

Amy and Jade decided to part company on Gehenna's first landing: the better to save time. Jade said, 'I'll search through those rooms towards the back.'

Amy replied, 'I'll check here, then make my way upstairs.'

'Don't go too far away, though; this place creeps me out.'

'Me, too,' Amy murmured. 'But look out for strange things, like false panels in the walls. Gaps behind tapestries or loose floorboards or secret doors.'

Jade's gaze flicked nervously towards Gehenna's bristling gloom.

'*Secret doors*. Whoopee-do … '

* * *

'So tell me about yourself,' said Daniel. 'Do you have a boyfriend waiting at home?'

Caroline said, 'No, not really. I do have a friend of sorts, but we're not all that close. In fact, we're cooling off. He's something of a jerk, actually, he keeps turning up with drugs and shouting, 'Here's the truth!' I don't quite understand that … '

'Nor me,' Daniel murmured.

'I'm not sure that *he* does. Like I say, he's a jerk.'

'Then why go out with him?'

'Because there's no one else. At least – nobody so far … '

* * *

While this gentle ardour brewed below, tension was on the boil in the eerie rooms above. At some point Jade had lost track of where Amy had gone. She'd bypassed her in the gloom and climbed one too many flights of the steep, creaking stairs. Found herself all alone on the dark attic floor with just a wall candle for support.

Jade had never been this far before although she'd heard all the details described in one of Lou's reports. So vividly had Lou explained the 'camping room' that Jade could picture it.

One aspect of that whole incident puzzled Jade: the fact that Amy thought she had been guided there by a shape which had disappeared. In all that had happened since, that alarming proposition had been somehow overlooked.

Was it just possible that there was someone else lurking inside the house? Might they use secret doors?

Or could the entire thing be ascribed to one of Amy's wilder, more colourful ideas?

Jade tugged at the attic door. As it eased open a little she peered cautiously inside. It was difficult for her to see very much; there was no light in the room. The hall candle lacked the strength to cast its light that far. She backtracked to the shallow niche where its thick stump was wedged and pulled it free from its hold.

Clutching it fervently, as though it were some kind of magic talisman designed to ward off harm, she returned to the heavy door and stepped inside. She stopped the door from closing, just in time.

Exactly as had been described, Gehenna's strange 'treasure trove' unfolded before Jade's eyes. She wandered amongst it all, touched clothes and old map books. Fingered rusting penknives, copper farthings, birchwood crooks. Played on a tin whistle, tried on a crushed felt cap, felt guilty, snatched it off.

But – ever drawn on – Jade's gaze suddenly fixed on a strip of white calico which had been roughly tacked to a wall. Faintly, beneath the cloth, she could discern the lines of what looked like a door.

So smoothly did the concealed door yield to Jade's first nervous touch that she practically flew inside. She barely saved herself from pitching down the throat of a hungry, draughtless shaft which waited just beyond. A shaft so dark and deep that it surely had to lead straight down to Hell itself.

Yet Jade still ventured on. It was as if the very air of the place had drugged her mind.

Though claustrophobia was tightening her chest, she made her cautious way down crudely fashioned steps. Through an atmosphere so still that the flame of the candle barely flickered at all. Down, almost vertically – towards Gehenna's roots. Past quiet, deserted rooms which were just visible at certain points.

All the time closing in on a stench of such an obscene nature that it caused her stomach muscles to clench …

35

'Of course, when we leave here,' said Daniel, we'll each head off to our own separate lives. You'll go back to your home and I'll return to mine. You'll be in Nottingham, while I'll be on the farm.'

'Which is just a train journey. Or two hours in a car ... '

'That's true.'

'Which is not that long.'

Daniel said, 'Are you inviting me to come and visit you?'

Caroline laughed. 'Well I'm not telling you to push off! Of course you'll visit me, won't you?'

Daniel's eyes shone. 'Yes, sure. I'd be honoured ... '

* * *

Though romance might be in the air inside the quiet kitchen, it had failed to spread elsewhere.

Poor Jade was flagging. Her perilous descent had sucked all the strength from her legs, and fired starbursts in her brain. Every muscle was tense, each nerve was at full stretch and she was filled with regret.

She should have turned back but the interminable climb seemed too much to attempt when she was all but spent. What she really required was an exit point of sorts: a door, or gaping crack.

So far she had seen none, but then, she'd not seen much: the smoky candle's light barely reached past her face. All she could do was hope, continue down the shaft and pray its end would arrive.

At last the decline ceased. The tight, compressed sides widened into a room. By Jade's best estimate, the chamber was well-removed from the main part of the house, located perhaps near the rear yard. Not one glimmer of light had the strength to reach that far. No sound could pierce the walls. Worse, when the room was built, its shelves and cupboards fixed, its floorboards nailed in place, its ceiling crudely smoothed, two things were overlooked: the kind of fitments which would have helped. It had no windows, and no door.

With the candle failing fast, Jade searched amongst the shelves for a functioning lantern. She eventually found one: a half-filled hunter's lamp, so old its brass was green with mould and verdigris.

She lifted the smoke-stained glass, held a match to the thin mantle and raised the lantern aloft.

A pale light blossomed, and Jade took a longer look at the cluttered, fusty room in which she had ended up.

She decided it must be a workroom of some kind: a resting place for junk. All kinds of pots, jars, old tools and knotted string were heaped on sagging shelves, or spilled from open drawers. A rich mixture of scents - beeswax, camphor and grease - hung heavy on the air.

Coming from beneath her, Jade detected a faint draught. A breeze as cold as ice, stinking of fungus and earth. She pulled back a mildewed fibre sack and found herself looking at a heavy trapdoor.

Jade fervently believed that the three locks on the trapdoor were not for decorative purposes. They were there for a purpose: that the trap should remain shut. Only the truly brave or reckless would proceed. Only the truly blind would fail to spot the faint, brown aura of evil. For evil is tangible - Jade was convinced of that. Evil gives off a smell of ruin and decay. Evil lurks in the dark and has roots deep in the earth. Evil has a brain, motive and soul …

She stooped to spread the piece of sacking back in place and caught the softest sound. It was so gentle, Jade had to hold her breath in order to be sure she'd genuinely heard: it was like a snowflake's cough, or the snoring of a moth in a distant room.

She glanced around her, trying to locate the source. But Jade knew all along that it rose up through the floor. She got down to her knees and lowered her cautious face until her dark hair brushed the boards.

Something shifted below the floor, then painfully hauled itself across a bed of straw. Jade heard coarse breathing - a murmur - half a curse. She heard the clink of chains, of links scrapping on a wall. Her heart beat like a drum: she thought that she had found out what happened to Lou.

'Lou, are you down there?' All signs of movement ceased. The only sounds Jade heard came from her own lips. She hissed, 'Are you okay?'

After a lengthy pause, a man's voice whispered, 'Who is there?' It was a tired voice, cracking, desperately old. It was the kind of voice Methuselah might have had. Hoarse and low and hesitant, as if it was unused to formulating words.

Spreadeagled on the floor, with her face pressed to the cold boards, Jade listened with dismay. At first reluctant to trust a stranger's voice, the man below at last deemed her 'not of the curse'. She was not one of those sent to torment his soul with promises of release.

He croaked, 'Such torment!'

'Not this time,' said Jade. 'I'm a friend.'

The man said, 'I have no friends, only the doomed and lost. If you have a soul you should flee, for each moment you tarry is a hazard too many. He will cast you down here to join us – '

'Join with who?'

'The corpses slick with worms, and those poor souls still alive.'

'Is there a girl down there? A new one, just arrived?'

'There may be,' said the man. 'I heard some moaning and sobbing, late last night. She dwells in the next cell – unconscious, I suspect. She has been hushed for several hours, but may be still alive. I doubt he's slain her yet. That is not his way, child – he will want to break her will: make her so terrified that she will lose all control. When your friend is at her worst – and every hope is dashed – he will glory in her pain.'

'This is impossible!' cried Jade, shocked and afraid.

'Speak softly, child,' he hissed, 'or the fiend himself may hear. Around these dungeons 'tis not wise to catch his eagle eye nor tweak his bat-like ear … '

Jade tried to calm her thoughts: to settle on a course of sensible action. It was far from easy: ideas were blinking out like stars leaving the sky at the finish of time. All that remained was a massive void: a silent, blank canvas where once ideas had been. Jade could not handle such trauma on her own: she needed strength and help, someone to take control. All she could come up with was how good it would be to turn into somebody else.

'I'll have to fetch some help,' she said. 'I have three friends in the house – '

'Don't go – you shan't return!'

'I will – I promise.'

'Promising is not enough. We have been vowed to before, and always were forsook. Besides, the very act of movement may attract the thing which you most fear. He may be waiting to claim you, right outside. The moment you depart you may seal your own fate. You may be forced to join us in this awful world – where the fiend drinks our blood … '

Scarcely able to believe the things that she was hearing, Jade questioned her own mind. Had she gone crazy – had she made all this up? Was she hopelessly trapped in some insane nightmare? Had she created this 'fiend' who dragged people away and survived by drinking blood? Her limbs were shaking like saplings in a gale. Her throat and mouth were dry, her eyes were saucer-wide. She could not even scream: she thought that if she screamed the hordes of Hell might hear.

'I don't know what to do. I'm scared that if I leave he will capture me too. Or if I stay here he'll catch me just the same. Or maybe he'll kill Lou the moment I am gone. I ought to rescue you, or something – I don't know. My mind's a total wreck.'

'Do not give up, child – don't let me dull your resolve! Sometimes the monster sleeps, and that sleep may last for days. Sometimes he will disappear in search of fresher prey. That, too, will occupy his time.'

'How will we know, though?'

'It is silent down here now. There is no sign that he is around, no footsteps, and no one screams. But we are shackled here and there is naught that we can do – '

Jade said, 'I'll try to help … '

She hunted for the keys which would release the trapdoor's locks and free those trapped below. She searched through a multitude of boxes, jars and tins. Combed through myriad shelves and scoured cupboards, on her knees. Frantic, but desperately trying to keep down the noise so that *he* – the monster - would not hear.

But the more Jade hunted, so the closer she was drawn into the heartless web of ultimate defeat.

She could not find the keys.

They *had* to be in there – she had to keep looking. All the while losing precious time …

* * *

Meanwhile, in the world outside, another scene unfurled, one in which fiends played little part. Wholly oblivious to what was occurring in the depths of Gehenna, Caroline and Daniel were walking in the fog, in need of space and time which were in short supply indoors where Franklin and Martha lurked. The pair were like spellbound lovers as they strolled around the outside of the house and they paid no heed at all to the restrictions on their sight. Fog cannot thwart the course of courtship's starry path when such starlight compensates …

Caroline said, 'It must be that pressure and stress can somehow condense time.'

Daniel said, 'In English?'

'Well. We've only just met - and yet it somehow seems as if we've already been friends for years. As if you were always there – lingering just out of sight – and now I've seen your face.' She turned to stare at him. 'Like people in war situations. One famous writer wrote a whole book about it.'

'Did he?'

'The life and times of people under strain.'

'I've never heard of it.'

'That's not the title, idiot!' Caroline touched his arm. The kind of careless touch old friends give all the time. And yet it was as if she'd triggered an alarm – or received a mild shock.

'I can't stop thinking about you,' she murmured. 'When you're not in my sight I wonder where you are. And I wonder if, perhaps, you are thinking of me too – and if you're missing me.'

She whispered, 'Are you?'

Daniel took her in his arms. He bent towards her face and gently nuzzled her lips. He said, 'The missing never stops. I miss you all the time – '

Caroline locked her arms around him …

After a timeless span the pair eased themselves apart, the way new lovers do. The strength and potency of their embrace left them breathless: they had to turn away to organize their thoughts. They stared off into space to still their racing hearts and cool their tingling lips. But something unspoken made them return as one, made them renew their pledge with one more crushing kiss. Made them practically swoon – made the blood race through their veins as though it was riding on fire.

This time, when they parted, there was a different sense: one of affirmation. They were not mistaken in believing that first kiss was just the opening salvo in a long kissing exchange; there would be more to come – longer, deeper, softer kisses – kisses born of the soul. For each had found someone amidst that lugubrious wrack of fog, sinister hosts, and rooms founded on gloom. Someone who would fill their dreams with passion, warmth and love and chase all nightmares away.

They walked on, arms entwined; stopped, and embraced again. Wholly surrounded now by the foul stench of the swamp, they had paused right at its rim and its ooze strained towards their feet. But perched on tough bristling tussocks they were framed like two statues, almost oblivious to the world around them.

Yet the swamp persisted – needled at them, and probed. Ribbons of natural methane gas writhed snake-like past their lips. It was a true killjoy. Like some jilted suitor it fumed with impotent rage.

'This whole place … ' Daniel said. 'The stench and endless fog. It's enough to drive you insane. It's sinister the way the fog just hangs in the air – so cold and wicked and intense. It's as if the very soul of that morbid old house is personified in its surroundings.'

Caroline said, 'That's like Jade-talk! Jade's really taken up with essences and souls – spirits in air and rock. She stares up at the stars, peers into moonlit wells. Talks about chakras, and chants weird mantras. I suppose it helps her, and it does seem to work. Most of the time she's very calm and controlled. It would take a lot to get her distressed. She's very composed and serene … '

* * *

'Got you!' Jade spat the words through teeth so tightly clenched they made her whole jaw ache. She snatched a key ring from a dusty, wooden tray and hurried across the room to the ominous trapdoor. She threw herself on her knees, and hissed, 'I've found the keys!' to the trapped man below.

The man warned, 'Tread carefully – do not dare to relax. You will betray our game if the fiend hears your voice.'

'Don't worry,' Jade replied. 'I'm certain we're all right. Everything's calm up here.'

'As it is down here, child – which means he's not around. This is the time to act! 'Tis brave hearts which secure the prize!'

'Just got to find the right keys - ' Jade fumbled with the tangled bunch. 'Just a few moments more and you'll be out … '

The final padlock clicked. Jade eased it from its hasp. Set it down on the floor. She straddled the heavy trapdoor and grasped at its large iron ring. Pulled up with all her strength as her legs locked in support. The muscles in her back and the tendons down her spine bulged as if they might explode. And though at first immovable, the trapdoor suddenly eased. It started to rise up, like the flat lid of a tomb. A gust of noisome air escaped, explored the room and came back to numb Jade's throat.

She lowered the ancient lamp into the yawning void which had appeared below. There was not much to be seen except a terrible gloom and a flight of wooden steps which spiralled out of sight. Each step bore long, deep cuts as if a beast had clawed at them in fits of rage. There was no sign of prisoners, nor corpses, nor iron chains. No hint of sound emerged: nothing disturbed the air. Jade gingerly advanced. The staircase swayed and creaked. She whispered, 'I'm coming down.'

The descent lasted for an age. It seemed impossible for the steps to extend so far. The place was like a huge well: a breathing pit for Hell. The walls were lined with rock, rough-hewn and black as coal. Water had once streamed down them, but had been transformed into gleaming sheets of ice. Jade said, 'Where are you?' as she leaned over the low handrail which served to keep the flight marginally more secure. But although she strained for a reply, the only sound came from the groaning steps. 'I'm at the bottom now,' she whispered, when she at last reached the floor of the shaft.

'Which way should I go, though?' She was faced by four arched doors. Each opened on to a tract of impenetrable gloom.

'I don't know which one to take – do you know?'

In the absence of any response, Jade was obliged to pick one herself …

36

Caroline and Daniel moved away from the foul swamp, driven back by its stench. They wandered idly into a massive barn, one of a pair of barns set some way from the house. It contained an old tractor, some farm machinery and an immense mound of straw.

Daniel was compelled by a mischievous impulse to sprint across the barn and leap into the straw –

He quickly wished he hadn't.

He nearly broke his back as he came down on something hard.

'What is it?' Caroline asked.

Daniel pulled some straw away, to reveal a rusting wreck. An early model Ford, complete with running boards. It was in such a ruined state that it was practically beyond salvaging.

Moved to probe further, Daniel burrowed in the straw and was stunned to find two more rusting old cars.

Both genuine classics.

Both like the ruined Ford.

Decrepit and decayed.

* * *

Jade followed right behind the lantern's pallid light. Its thin rays illuminated a disgusting floor along which Jade was forced to walk. A floor awash with blood. Littered with skulls and bones. Animal and human.

Jade was so shell-shocked that she just plodded on, her brain virtually swamped and battling to believe.

Was she still on the earth or had she unwittingly blundered into some grim and obscene netherworld?

* * *

'In better condition these would be worth something,' Daniel said, of the cars. 'If they'd been properly looked after, instead of being simply dumped here.' He sounded almost indignant.

'Perhaps they didn't know. Or maybe they didn't care.'

'They should have realized! Why on earth *bury* them in all this filthy straw? They were bound to rot away – a fool would have known that.'

'So the two old folk are fools,' Caroline said, shrugging. It wasn't like that was a surprise.

* * *

Nightmarish were the sounds of footsteps in the dark. The fiend was on his way.

Stunning booms rang around Jade like the notes of a great death knell. They fell on her from both sides, from behind her, and in front. But Jade was so benumbed that she merely stood and stared, waiting to meet her fate.

For it had suddenly dawned on her that there were no prisoners chained below. She had been snared in a trap, like a fly caught in a web. The voice that she had heard was the voice of doom: the words were the deceitful fiend's words.

What would he look like when he came, would she know his face?

Would she have time to say, '*Please – I don't want to die!*'

Would she have any time at all in which to fight?

Would she –

But no.

The fiend crept up and struck her from behind …

37

Daniel and Caroline retraced their steps towards the brooding house and paused when they saw a shape loom at them from the murk.

It was a fraught Amy: breathless, anxious and tired. 'I've been looking all over,' she said, 'and Lou's not anywhere. And now Jade's vanished, too. I thought she'd gone on ahead, but never caught her up. Do you know what I feel like? One of those characters in a haunted house movie, where they vanish one by one. Until only two are left and you know that one of them must be responsible.'

She ran tense fingers through waves of tangled hair. 'Do you think I should try the moors and see if she's got stuck out there?'

Caroline shook her head decisively. 'All that would happen then is you would both wind up lost.'

Amy and Caroline returned to Gehenna; Daniel remained outside. He still felt curious about the hidden cars and wanted to search around some more, check on the other barns. He took his dog with him, as much for company as for any help she'd give.

But the girls were simply too tense, and wandered back inside. They scraped the mud off their boots and sat down by the kitchen fire.

The house was very quiet. There were no signs at all of its two main residents.

'Where do you think Jade went?'

'I don't know,' Amy said. 'But I don't think she's in the house.'

Neither did Caroline: there was something in the air. A coldness born of loss, silence formed by absence. The tension they'd endured seemed to have increasingly attuned other instincts.

They could now *feel* things, where once they'd have had to see. They knew when things were wrong without being told why. And things were badly wrong with their situation – fools could have told them that. But from sensing danger to knowing what to do is a wholly different matter.

After a while the dog wandered back, and Caroline saw her settle down on her straw bed in the porch. She clipped Jess's leash on then stared outside, at the fog. Evening was closing in, the colour of dead leaves. She glanced down at the dog. 'Is he still rooting around?' The dog wagged her thin tail.

'You must be hungry … ' She slipped back into the house. Returned with a massive bone – it looked like half an ox.

She placed it on the floor. Jess was so overjoyed she hardly knew where to start.

'It's getting dark now,' Caroline said, as she joined Amy by the fire. 'It will be time to eat soon.'

'I can live without that. Pale soggy cabbage that was probably harvested last year, and barely roasted meat. When we get back, mark my words, I'm really going to eat nothing but healthy food.'

'Me too,' said Caroline, as she glanced towards the door.

She felt a slight stirring of unease in her mind.

'Daniel's been gone a while.'

There was no sign of life outside. There was nothing but seething fog …

'They're not normal, you know.'

'Who?'

Amy gave a tut. 'Who do you think?' she sighed. 'Do you see that Martha? The way she hangs out round the halls. Always staring at us, like we're fish in a bowl. Always lurking in shade – sliding along the walls – never quite seen, never quite not seen.'

'She's probably nervous.'

'Oh grow up, Caroline. I don't know why you're on their side all the time. They're not two befuddled old dears - they're two evil old monsters who *know* what's going on. Don't say they're nervous, because they're laughing in their boots: the only nervous ones in this setup are us. Which is all down to them and the way they practically drool at us!'

Caroline said, 'That's nonsense, you're just getting upset – '

'No! This is not *upset* – my *upset* has been, and then left! What I am feeling now is genuine *alarm*. Those old people frighten me.'

Silence came from outside. The dog had suddenly ceased tearing at her bone. The two girls looked round. There was tension in the porch: Jess must have heard something unusual in the fog. She was slowly rising up, leaving her meal behind. Her hackles bristled like they were electrically charged.

As Caroline eased her creaking chair back, it triggered the dog. She sprang against her leash with a violence born of rage. Something out in the night was causing Jess to snarl like a chainsaw gone berserk.

Caroline cried, 'Daniel!' as she ran towards the door.

Amy raced at her heels, shouting, 'Unclip her lead!'

The instant she was released, Jess tore off through the fog, and the darkness snapped her up …

'Now what?' Caroline whispered when silence took the place of the dog's fast-fading rage. 'Should we go after her?'

'Not like this,' Amy said. 'It's time we had something so that we can fight back.' She dashed inside the house and returned with a wicked knife, saying, 'I feel better now.'

'Amy, you might kill someone! You could end up locked in jail – '

'Say it was self-defence – I'm not going out unarmed. My sister disappeared, closely followed by Jade. They're not claiming me next.'

The girls crept through the fog. Their vision was no use at all but other attributes were keen. Their increasing sixth sense knew silence not as a 'void', but as a pregnancy of noise poised to explode. In its depths beat a heart – perhaps even a soul. It lacked only life's light …

Of course, there was no light of any sort around but even light's absence did not render them blind. Currents inside the fog – tendrils slowly writhing – gave them a focal point.

Thus it was that, though all seemed impossibly obscure, the girls could still find the means to progress through the yard. Not by listening to their brains, but by listening to their hearts: trusting to their instincts.

'Anything up ahead?'

'Feels like we're near a barn,' Caroline said softly. 'I can sense its outline looming up on us now.'

'Any sign of the dog?'

'Nothing – no sight or sound.'

'We should have brought a lamp – '

'If we'd had more time, we could have brought armed guards.'

Just as she said that, Caroline froze on the spot. Walking right at her heels, Amy slammed into her.

'*Listen!*'

From inside the barn came the merest hint of sound. That of someone's hoarse breathing.

The tense girls eased their way between the wide doors of the barn. They were met by a muted glow. A small gas lantern was softly hissing on the floor, its ring of jaundiced light fell over trampled straw. The light could barely reach the massive barn's high walls: most of the place was swallowed by shade.

But, in one corner, the girls saw a prostrate form –

Directly behind that, eyes watched them from the gloom –

They flinched as the eyes advanced –

Relaxed as Jess appeared, half-slinking, tail wagging.

Caroline outran Amy and was the first to reach the motionless, silent shape. She stretched one hand down, gently touched Daniel's face. He stirred, his eyes opened, he coughed once, spat out blood. He glanced towards his thigh: the red stain on his jeans was not spilled ketchup.

'Someone attacked me!' he cried. 'I had no chance! It was all too sudden – did you see him outside?'

Caroline shook her head.

Daniel cursed. 'He was so strong. He had almost inhuman strength … '

38

With the two girls flanking him, Daniel limped slowly towards the blackness of the house. While he was walking he told them how he'd accidentally stumbled on someone in the barn. Someone curled in the straw. Somebody fast asleep. But who woke like a cat. Even as Daniel was recovering from the shock of finding him, the figure sprang upright and tried barging his way past. Daniel grabbed at his sleeve. The figure turned around and punched him full in the face. Startled but conscious, Daniel came fighting back. They grappled – hit the straw – rolled over – lashing out. (Real fights are far removed from those carefully mapped out for showing on-screen.)

'I had him pinned down but couldn't see his face. It was so dark, you see, and I couldn't hold him still. But I could tell that he was tough and brutish; possessed of phenomenal strength. He sent me sprawling with a straight thrust of his arm. I grabbed him round the neck and we crashed into the wall. That was when I got this wound –' Daniel gestured to his leg. 'Stabbed myself on a nail. Which made me stumble a little, so he turned and grabbed a plank of wood and crashed it down on my spine. When I collapsed on the dirt he grabbed me by the hair and smashed my face on his knee. Which almost did it: I could feel myself going. I made one last attempt to punch him but I only hit thin air. Next thing, everything was black. I was falling like a sack. The floor was my only friend.'

'Could it have been Franklin?' said Amy.

'Possibly. That old guy might be stronger than he looks, but the guy I fought seemed *big*. It was hard to tell for sure. It happened so suddenly. And things were too confused.'

'But he just left you there?'

Daniel said, 'It seems that way. And I was helpless then, he could have done as he pleased. In fact, as I recall, which isn't all that much, he did come back again. But not to hurt me, he came to bring the lamp. He set it on the floor as if to guide *you* there. I'm pretty vague on that; you can't think too clearly when your brains are in your feet. The sense I got, though, was that he wasn't really trying to damage me, more trying to get away. As though I'd frightened him. Like he was resting up and I almost trod on him.'

'Why should he want to do that?' said Amy. 'Guide us there?'

'I don't know. Guilt maybe – he really hit me hard. Even though he was holding back he used sufficient force to pummel me senseless.'

As they continued across the yard the moon broke through the clouds above the fog – producing a bizarre effect. A combination of the moonlight and the reflecting fog produced strange distortions in the motionless air. It seemed for a few moments as if the house assumed an almost ship-like shape. Its lofty gables gave the appearance of bowed sails. A minaret-like spire seemed to be a soaring mast. A squat tower at the easternmost corner of the house was like a forecastle looming over the yard. Just for an instant, from a window near the roof – probably in the attic – a gleam of light appeared. As if someone up there had lit a small lantern. But it quickly disappeared. And as suddenly as it arrived the ethereal glow dispersed, until everything appeared as before.

The three continued their journey to the house. They entered the dismal kitchen, where Caroline patched up Daniels's leg. When he tried his weight on it, it looked as much fun as balancing on a spike.

But at least Daniel was mobile, which was useful when someone close at hand was willing to pick fights.

He vowed next time he'd win.

Amy said, 'Sure you will. He caught you by surprise. And you've got us for back-up.'

Caroline checked the fire in the range. It was still burning strongly. She edged a little closer to its warmth.

'I wonder if it was Franklin,' she said, 'who lit the lamp up in the attic. We should go and talk to him, find out what's going on. Find what got into him if he beat Daniel up. Or, if it wasn't him, then who on earth was it? We really ought to know. Maybe there's someone else here – someone else hanging round. Maybe that someone else knows where Lou and Jade are!'

Amy said, 'Maybe the 'someone else' is in the attic now – and it's not Franklin at all ... '

39

The three made their way upstairs and crept into the dim attic, for which they had gone prepared. Each clutched a candle which helped to bolster their nerves. But each, unconsciously, held theirs out at arm's-length, as if it were a vampire-slaying cross. Not because they had expectations of meeting 'dark forces' – but it is a natural instinct to put faith in light: to send it on ahead and let it explore the nooks and crannies where fear lurks ...

Everything looked much the same to Amy's cautious eyes: nothing seemed to have changed. For her two companions, change wasn't an issue. They had not been there before, and had nothing to compare. But the sight of the huge haul of travellers' effects made them pull up short. What was it doing there – why gather such a hoard? Caroline had no idea but Daniel thought he knew. The idea in his brain spread icy tentacles, which chilled him to his core.

'About two years ago,' he said, 'a policewoman came to visit Wellbeck Farm. Someone had gone missing: a Danish hitchhiker. She was called Bibe Poppe – the name sticks in my mind. She set off from Blacktor, after telling some people there she'd head for Minetop next. She never got there, though, simply disappeared. After a fortnight passed, her family grew concerned. She used to call them regularly, once a week, but the calls suddenly stopped and they got no response when they tried calling her.'

Daniel stretched his injured leg out; his wound was stiffening up. He sat down on the edge of a table heaped with packs. He idly picked one up. Quite a distinctive one. Pink, bound with many straps.

'The policewoman had a photograph which she made us all look at. Showed it at every house and farmstead on the moor. A picture of the girl – pretty, chubby and blonde-haired – toting a pack like this. The pack was so unusual that I still remember it.'

He turned the pack around and slowly undid the straps.

Inside, amongst some clothes, toiletries and a plastic purse, was Bibe Poppe's passport ...

In the silence which followed, even a hamster's sneeze would have had the impact of a bomb. The sheer immensity of what had been revealed almost persuaded the three to take off for the hills. But in their present plight – with Daniel's injured leg – they'd not have got too far.

So much made sense, though, so much fell into place. The cars hidden in straw, the items in the loft. The disappearing girls ...

Could they – now they'd been warned – avoid a similar fate?

'They must be like the old wreckers who used to lure lost ships onto rocks,' Caroline said.

'No, not like wreckers,' said Daniel. 'Not so bold. They wouldn't take the risk of catching someone's eye. More sinister than that. They simply lie in wait, like spiders in a web. Sooner or later somebody will pass by – somebody seeking help, or merely passing the time. And once they've stepped inside they've entered a black hole. They're simply swallowed up.'

'What do they do with them?' said Amy. 'Murder them?'

Daniel said, 'I don't think they'd try to become friends.'

'But that means Lou and Jade – '

'Have probably vanished for ever,' Daniel said. 'Although it's possible that they are still alive, somewhere inside the house,' he went on. 'We can't be certain until – ' His voice dried up. He did not want to say 'till their corpses turn up'. 'They might simply be trapped – maybe tied up and gagged – '

'Not definitely dead!' This came from Amy, who snatched at the precious hope as though it was a line tossed to a drowning soul. She needed to believe, needed to find some strength to help her carry on. 'Some place we've not looked!'

'The cellar,' Daniel said. 'That's the only spot left – no one's explored it yet. And from what Franklin has said, it's one enormous maze. What better place could there be?'

The girls were anxious to set off right away, but Daniel held them back. He was not so reckless.

He said, 'It seems to me that in your eagerness you've overlooked something. What about Martha and Franklin? I don't think that they'll stand idly by while we conduct our search. Those two aren't on our side so they won't offer much help: rather the opposite. We'll have to sneak down and one of us should stay outside to get the others out if anything goes wrong. The last thing we need is for all of us to end up trapped in some hole under the ground ... '

40

Amy crouched inside a pool of gloom next to the cellar door. She scanned the empty hall. Nothing was moving, nobody made a sound. Gehenna was completely still; devoid of signs of life. If that monstrous couple prowled, they must have learned to survive without a need for breath. That very silence was what frightened Amy most. It was not born of peace, but of tension, dread and threat. It felt so overwound she feared the slightest shift might spring it back to life ...

Nor did Amy quake alone for, just beyond the cellar door, her friends appeared to be rooted to the spot. Their bold invasion of the labyrinthine world took on a fresh aspect once they passed its threshold. What courage they possessed drained faster than a tap turned to maximum flow. They both felt daunted, helpless, and ludicrously small - like two young rabbits trapped in a fox's earth.

'I wish I'd kept the shotgun,' Daniel said. 'Naturally Franklin stashed it away. I still have some cartridges – ' He groped in one of the pockets of his hunter's jacket. 'For all the use they are right now they might as well be made of wood. I'd trade them in for a decent catapult.'

'Things might not come to that,' Caroline said. 'Look at the odds here: we're both young, fit and strong. Martha must weigh a hundred and twenty kilos while Franklin's just skin and bone. How much harm can they do?'

Daniel did not feel encouraged.

He said, 'Enough to fill that loft with all that stuff ... '

They searched through the first dim tract of that spider's web-like maze somewhat half-heartedly. They did not expect to find any signs of bodies there; they would probably lie further in. The further the better – more concealed from prying eyes. Probably so far within that people would abandon the search before they chanced on them.

No, the pair would have to march on; walk beyond that yawning arch which marked the real beginning of that grim and hateful realm. Step forward hand in hand so that, if things went wrong, they would not die alone ...

41

'The shotgun!' Caroline gasped. 'It's over there behind those logs!'

Daniel almost wept with relief. He snatched up the weapon, snapped it open and felt relief spread like a wave of fire through his trembling hands. The gun appeared intact. Everything was in place, No vital parts had been destroyed.

He took two cartridges from his pocket, slotted them into the firing chamber and slammed the barrels back into place.

He felt like a different person. Felt – for the very first time – that they might just have a chance …

Bolstered by the retrieval of the gun, the pair moved swiftly on: searching, praying, hoping.

Though they did not know it, they were on the same route that Lou had walked. They were treading the selfsame ground that led to her fate. They were seeing the same wall lamps, now glimmering again. They were hearing similar heart-thuds.

But they travelled faster than Lou – despite Daniel's limp - for they were not alone, and there was more urgency manifested in their stride. They were trying to save two friends who might still be alive, and time was not on their side.

Their pace slowed dramatically when they approached the grim stretch of rooms that had caused Lou such distress.

The gruesome area had the same effect on them. It made their blood run cold and chilled them right to their souls. The array of manacles, altars and chopping blocks was a disquieting sight.

As, too, were the paintings which they saw daubed on the walls: tableaux depicting scenes of horrific torment.

Ritual practices were frequently portrayed – hinting at an occult intent.

Moving rapidly on, the pair probed deeper still. Dungeons came; dungeons passed.

They reached a tract of darkness – devoid of any lamps. At the far end just a hint, no more, of cautious light. A light that might emerge blinking, rubbing its eyes, after years in the dark.

And a guttural chanting: the unconscious, dull refrain of someone barely aware that they produced a noise. Perhaps someone whose thoughts were fully focused on an all-engrossing task.

The gleaming shotgun shook in Daniel's tense white hands as he led Caroline along the sonorous shaft.

Cold water dripped on them from the curving roof above. Fly pupae cracked and burst on the rough ground underfoot. The gleam ahead deepened, took on a ruby hue, as if its fuel were blood.

They stopped one metre away from the doorway to the room which gave birth to the sound.

There could be no turning back now, no time for second thoughts –

How could they walk away, having progressed this far?

They had to see this through and confront what was in the room.

Find out what made it chant.

Caroline gnawed at her lip as Daniel's tense body advanced the final step. She moved beside him as he froze in the wide doorway. He dropped the shaking gun so she stooped to pick it up. As she rose her eyes caught sight of what was in the room, and she bit down on a scream.

Desiccated human corpses were hanging from the walls.

The body of a sheep was staked out on the floor.

Rummaging through its entrails – as if seeking something – was a huddled, intent form …

An awful silence descended as the morbid chanting stopped, and the rummager looked round.

It gazed right at them, with eyes of ruby fire –

Breath hissed from its lips in a low, threatening hiss –

It started to advance – giving no time at all for them to form a plan …

They fled as best they could, not aided in the least by the wound to Daniel's leg.

No time for firing the half-forgotten gun –

No thoughts of reasoning with what raced behind –

Hardly a thought in their heads at all –

Only a desperate urge to escape …

42

'I'm not going to make it like this,' Daniel gasped. 'The pain in my leg's getting worse all the time. Go on ahead - I'll be all right.'

Caroline refused the idea point-blank, but Daniel pushed her on.

'I'm going to use the gun and force the thing to hold back. You get back to the house and I'll follow behind. Wait by the cellar door. The moment I'm through, slam it and throw the bolts.'

'And if you don't arrive?'

'I promise you I will. I swear it in my heart. I swear it on my life – '

Caroline paused, caught in two minds.

'You have to go and warn Amy. You can't let this thing catch her by surprise.'

So finally Caroline ran – tears streaming down her face – a huge lump in her throat. She had such harrowing visions in her mind: visions that were being fuelled and nurtured by every fear she had ever known. Visions of pain and death, of torture and torment, of darkness and despair.

She saw the two of them lying on the floor –

Pictured them opened up – their vital organs exposed –

Imagined the dreadful beast which prowled that tunnel world feasting, tucking into their flesh ...

* * *

The moment Caroline left, Daniel turned to face his doom, fearful, but not unbowed, He wedged the shotgun against his right shoulder, braced his legs. He raised the long barrels, squinted down them, locked his arms. Dreamed he was on his local shooting range awaiting the next clay pigeon. Then cleared all thoughts from his mind.

He needed one shot, that was all: just one clear open shot. Enough to slow the thing down, make it stop in its tracks. Just one shot down the shaft, which held a perfect line.

But he waited just too long ...

43

At least a shot was fired – and the entire labyrinth started like a jack-in-the-box.

The stunning discharge, trapped in the confined space, transferred its energy into an expansive shock wave. It hurtled down the shaft, caught up with Caroline and made her innards contract.

She glanced behind her, slowed her pace down and prayed he'd come. Prayed that she would see Daniel in the distance, safe and sound.

But when the tunnel lamps showed an approaching shape, it was definitely not Daniel's ...

The shot's diminishing roar still had sufficient strength to make it to the house. Amy was electrified when she heard it and grabbed the door. She whipped it back so hard she pulled tendons in her arm. She squinted through the murk, not certain what she would see or what she hoped to find.

At first there was nothing – then the small, distant form of Caroline appeared, sprinting, all on her own. Nobody else. Nobody close behind.

Most of all, no Daniel ...

'Lock it,' Caroline gasped, when at last she emerged into Gehenna's hall. 'Make sure it's bolted.'

'Daniel's still inside!'

'Daniel's not coming out – I don't think he's survived. There's something in the shafts ... He tried to slow it down but it keeps on coming.'

'Do you mean it killed him – murdered him just like that?'

'It might kill all of us, Amy, it's not done yet. I don't know what we'll do. If a shotgun can't stop it, what chance have we two got?'

The pair almost hit the roof when the stalker suddenly attacked the cellar door. Over and over, he slammed it with his fists. The entire hallway shook and echoes reached to the roof. A concentrated rage emerged as muffled howls interspersed with grunting.

And then came another sound – behind them, down the hall. The girls swivelled as one and saw Franklin at the kitchen door. He was grinning like a wolf. The faintest of chuckles emerged from his dry throat.

'Why are you doing this?' cried Amy. 'Why pick on us?'

Franklin's thin, bloodless lips twitched like worms around his teeth.

'To preserve my line, and keep the old blood alive. To feed my great ancestor ... '

The girls raced up the stairs, locked themselves in the poor haven of their bedroom.

They felt anything but secure there – but it was the only refuge they had left. At least their belongings were near: they might die feeling at home.

Precious few hopes remained, for the beast would surely come.

Franklin would see to that ...

44

But nothing gave pursuit; nothing raced up the stairs; nothing attacked the door.

An eerie silence replaced the sounds of rage – a silence so intense they could have punched a hole through it. Gehenna held its breath. Not one loose floorboard creaked. Not one nervous throat coughed. The only disruption came from two pounding hearts, from the rasping of tight breath and from the wiping of damp palms. Sounds which were miniscule when set against that gargantuan quietness.

'What do you think is happening?' breathed Amy, when her fraying nerves threatened to tear apart. 'That door won't stop him: the frame's rotting away. Hiding behind these beds won't hold him up for long. Why hasn't he attacked us? What is he waiting for? Why is everything so quiet?'

Caroline had no answers, only the same questions, but said, 'It must give him a thrill knowing he's in control. Making his victims sweat – like a cat with a mouse – getting high on their fear. Why should he end this? He would miss out on his fun. He could keep us trapped for days; we're not going anywhere. He's probably stopped off to plot his next few moves with Martha and Franklin.'

'That evil pair must have planned all this,' said Amy, 'from the start. Pretending they took us in from the goodness of their hearts. We should have suspected – '

'I think we did, Amy. But we were too scared to believe …'

Minutes which felt like years trudged remorselessly by, and still that silence prowled. It was like a shrewd beast hovering outside their door, tempting them to go out, urging them to look. Its message seemed to be: 'I might have gone away – see if the coast is clear.'

But the two dared not risk it, although they considered it: weighed up the likelihood of being able to spring a surprise. Pictured running down the stairs – tearing along the hall – bursting past the front door.

It wasn't such a good idea that they felt moved to try. Even if they broke out how much could they achieve? They had been thwarted before, why should the shrouding fog be any better disposed to them now?

'I'm getting hungry,' said Amy. 'We missed out on our tea.'

'You can't think about food at a moment like this!'

'What should I think about then? My stomach's going wild. It needs some calming down.'

'Think about good things, think about getting out. Think how happy we'll be when we get safely home.'

'I'd rather think of food, I've got some chance of that.'

'Don't be such a pessimist ... '

But pessimism grew as the long impasse went on, with no relief in sight. In fact, things worsened, for – as the minutes passed – the few candles in the room took turns to sputter out: mere stumps when the ordeal began, they quickly worked their way through their small reserves of wax.

As the pale flames dwindled, the shadows in the room appeared as threatening clumps which inexorably converged. Niches turned into holes; holes turned into deep caves in which monsters might lurk. And, since total darkness has no clear boundaries, the limits of the room slowly began to fade. The ceiling disappeared as though it had been absorbed into a greater void.

This was so mesmerizing that – when the walls merged too – many overwrought thoughts found themselves dragged behind. It was hard for the girls to stay keyed up and at their peak; their senses became numbed. Tension is draining, adrenalin is a spur which soon demands a toll: its appetite is immense.

Though the girls still felt vigilant, their focus had become less intense. Through inattention they lost that vital edge which separates success from second best. And as their exhausted minds wandered and their concentration roved, both of the girls missed something.

It was the furtive sound of stone scraping on stone, with agonizing slowness. In the depths of the cavernous fireplace a door was opening on enormous iron hinges which had been freshly oiled: a door of huge stone blocks, stained by years of fires and fit to seal up a tomb. Beyond it showed more darkness, a darkness so complete that even in that room its black visage stood out. With eternity for its root, and oblivion as its goal. And nothingness between.

Something began to move – soft, stealthy, deliberate: but still the girls missed it. They were counting heartbeats, or flickers, or murmurs in their minds. Thoughts on a different plane: conscious yet not watchful. Numbed by that silent room in which they had nothing on which to fix their eyes.

Frightened and weary – cold, hungry and alone.

Resigned merely to wait until someone made a move.

Devoid of hopes and plans: their initiative destroyed by inactivity ...

But the girls certainly remembered how to shriek when someone struck a match, and light flared in the room. Framed by the great hearth was the figure of a man. His clothes were disgusting rags and his face a tense grey slab. His hair a tangled mass, like a frost-streaked auburn thatch. An enormous hand, reaching towards them -

But not to touch them: rather to suppress their screams.

His every move displayed a tension and unease.

His voice was a desperate plea to not give him away.

His fear was palpable.

'No one must know,' he hissed, 'that I have come to your room, or every hope is dashed. My name is Lucien, I am Franklin's grandson. I wish to give advice – for what use my words may have. But you must first trust me and vacate this death trap room to talk with me a while. We must flee through the priest holes and the false walls from the past – ' He pointed to the hearth, to the great darkness beyond. 'I have my own room down there – a place so miserable that even Franklin shuns it.'

What had the girls got to lose? To stay was to face certain doom, trusting the man was just a risk. It took moments for them to give their word that they would not scream out or in any way alert Franklin to what Lucien proposed: that he would shelter them and offer them what help he was able to provide.

So he proceeded to lead them from the trap that was their room through narrow passageways in Gehenna's ancient walls. Rarely speaking a word. Never showing a light. Never once looking back.

Speed would prove vital if the girls were to survive. Every moment was valuable – every movement must count. Neither had any doubt that their entire existence was hanging by a thread ...

Once inside a squalid room in a quiet corner of the house, Lucien's nerves relaxed a little. He lit a lantern and winced as the two girls gagged on the disgusting air and eyed the refuse on the floor. He said, 'I have little choice, for to keep this place I cannot tend to it. I can neither air it nor clean it, or I would surely catch Franklin's eye and then incur his wrath. The only peace that I can find is when I'm so silent he overlooks me. These days I am so unimportant to Franklin that he is content to leave me on my own, to my own devices. Which means that while he is diverted elsewhere we will have time to debate your plan – assuming you have made a plan.'

'We were rather hoping that you had one,' said Amy.

Lucien flinched. 'I did invent plans once, but they've been left behind. Let us hope we can find one now. In the meantime I shall talk a while. Bear with me if I lapse ... '

While they listened, rigid as statues, Lucien told the girls everything that he knew. It was a slow task, for it quickly became clear that Lucien was not a fit and healthy man. He had a rare condition which was destroying his brain, a section at a time. Though he was lucid at times, and fully rational, he would without warning drift away and grapple to locate his thoughts. His head and limbs would twitch as though they were on strings over which he had no control. Though Lucien fought against this, the battles were short-lived. Always that void returned, always the silence came. A silence which foretold the life he had in store – for his illness had no cure.

'I tried to warn you off,' he said, 'as best I could – but it was clearly not enough. I tried in the large barn – ' He looked at Caroline - his pallid, craggy face oddly soft and childlike. 'That was me on the roof. But the rotted bough fell and I damaged several ribs.'

As if to confirm this – perhaps to make the point that he was on their side, and not part of a ruse – he raised his tattered shirt, growling against the pain, to show livid bruising. He had yet more wounds stretching towards his back. Amy made him turn around so that she could take a better look. She saw that his entire back was a furious nightmare of seeping crimson weals.

Amy said, 'Who did this?'

'Grandfather,' Lucien said. 'That was my punishment for daring to interfere. As soon as he found out he beat me with a lash. Led me beyond the barns so that you would not hear if I chanced to cry out. My grandfather despises me because of my illness. He says that I am insane and will not long survive. Which means that centuries of service and planning will simply pass away. All that he has taught me – all he's tried to preserve – is fading with the brain which is my hope and curse. For despite his best efforts, I – like my own mother – will escape him into death.

'My mother ran away the first chance that she had – horrified by her fate. She eloped with a simple farmhand who occasionally helped out on our land. They went to a small village – near Bedford, I believe. There they forged a new life and strove to forget their past to leave their nightmares behind. They worked quite hard, too: laboured every hour they could. Yet they had so few skills, and no 'manners' to fit in. They had seldom been taught much: places remote as this do not put schooling first.

'They did succeed, though, in acquiring a kind of home – a ramshackle affair – little more than a shack. Which is where I was born. Where I took my first steps. Where I thought 'family' meant 'safe'.

'And they had such dreams there – such hopes and futile plans. At times they did believe that they had left Gehenna's reach. But it came to them one dark night with a tumour in its hand, and struck my father down.'

'So you and your mother came back here?' said Amy.

Lucien sighed. 'Soon after father died. There was no alternative that the poor woman could see. She knew she'd had her chance – such things don't come again. Gehenna's like a drug: once it infects your veins it is hard to give it up. She returned reluctantly, yet came back nonetheless. I was only four years old, yet even then was lost. When my mother expired of a broken heart and soul, I lost my only support.'

'Franklin and Martha raised you?'

'If raising's what it was. They offered me this life – ' Lucien said bleakly, and his sad, tormented gaze took in the few pitiful things which he'd smuggled into his room.

He had some candles, three glasses, several books, a small bundle of clothes, a photograph or two, an ancient radio, a pair of nail scissors, a hairbrush and a flask.

These were the forlorn relics of a life doomed from the start. A life over which he himself had little control. A life from which his disease – his Huntington's chorea – would soon release him.

45

After a sustained and particularly violent bout of uncontrolled jerking, a weakened Lucien returned to his tale. He told the two girls about the days of Lord Cornwell, of the search for missing priests, of Agnes and Robert. Told how the pair had fought against insuperable odds to establish their own world. Told about darkness and torment, bugs and rats. Described squeezing water from dank soil to survive. Spoke of the feared Black Death, and the havoc it wrought. Told of how *they did not die* ...

'Nobody quite knows how, but despite the plague and the time my ancestors did manage to somehow stay alive. Franklin believes it was because they were 'selected', because they swore a pact with powers inside the earth – forces as old as time. Forces stirred by the act of digging in their realm, and the seduction of light. Vampires and werewolves, possibly wraiths and ghouls. Terrible, jealous beasts which carouse in the soil. Beings filled with envy and which desire the means to exchange their world for ours ...

'Whether this tale is true I am unable to say, but my forebears *did* survive. They could not have done so, of course, without great aid. Assistance from above: protectors, friends and slaves. People to bring them food, since the pair soon devoured what life crawled through the soil. Also equipment and tools to build their home, to provide protection and support from any outside prying eyes. To serve them all their days. The generations since. The offspring of the damned.' Lucien tended to the lamp. Its mantle was so frayed that it barely clung to life. He took a long draught of water from the flask – talking was thirsty work for one without much practice. He passed the flask to the girls, and they both managed a sip. Polite right to the end ...

'Of course, the offspring toiled only because they were promised a great reward. What they were offered was the chance of eternal life – a life they will enjoy when darkness rules the earth. A darkness which will rise when Robert peels the veils from his infernal arts. I deem this unlikely, but my relatives believe. Martha and my grandfather still hold on to their faith. They think if they toil enough – and if they contribute the flesh – then darkness will emerge.

'For in the flesh lies the germ – the marrow of the art – the core of all belief. Robert believes that the purpose of flesh is to conceal. The key to life itself resides in the mortal soul. And Robert sees the soul as something whole and real, not some arcane concept. He believes it can be exposed when the flesh is peeled away and those with eyes to see will recognize its shape. He believes that if he can find a soul, it will restore his youth – for even he grows old. And if he finds two he can restore to life the body of Agnes, who appears now to have died. She vanished years ago when a tunnel roof collapsed, and has never re-emerged. This is why Franklin toils so hard: he is searching for her corpse. He also believes he is close to being granted his reward. My grandfather is convinced that Robert is on the verge of extracting human souls … '

'And where do you fit in?' said Amy.

Lucien shrugged. 'I have no place in this. I have been a failure since the day that I was born. My grandfather is ashamed of me for having my disease. He curses me because it renders me too weak to help in his work. Nor does he trust me – he doubts that I have 'faith'. He fears I might betray the secrets of our life. This is why I am kept from 'visitors' – he fears I will bare the truth.'

Caroline said, 'All the people who've been killed here to further the 'art' – surely the police must have enquired?'

Lucien nodded, then paused to muster his strength. He had seldom talked so much in his thirty-five years. He said, 'The police *have* been on more than one occasion, but old people can lie. The things that you have seen have been accumulated over many years. Some, over centuries. It is not a weekly event, to kill someone. In truth such deaths are rare, with many years between. Most of what Robert does he inflicts on livestock. This was once a working farm and we still rear some sheep and cattle on the land. So yes, the police come, although infrequently. And what would they suspect of 'harmless' old people. They would hardly conceive that Franklin and Martha are two mass murderers! My grandfather is polite to them – helpful, caring and kind. Anyone can wear a mask should a real need arise. Few things are better versed in the concealment of evil than evil itself. It has, I must say though, been much harder of late. People these days have cars, which are more difficult to destroy. If the police should call again and probe inside the barns, their views are sure to change.'

'Can we not get away?' said Amy.

'It is too late – Robert would hunt you down. He is feeling strong now, fortified by his hope. Even now he prepares for the extraction of your souls. When all is set in place, he and my grandfather will break into your room. They will overpower you, or so my grandfather believes. He is not yet aware that you have been removed. My grandfather feels secure. It would not cross his mind that I would dare to intervene.'

'What of our friends, Lucien?'

That was the big question they'd not yet dared to ask.

Lucien looked uncomfortable – he did not want to add any more to the burden of grief that they already had. He craved some better news to pass on but life was not disposed to hope and miracles.

He said, 'They will be somewhere in the labyrinth below. Either already dead, or destined to die soon.'

'But possibly still alive?'

Lucien gave a shrug.

'It is unlikely,' he said.

46

If there was the remotest chance that their three friends were still alive, the girls would have to check. Lucien was vehemently opposed to this, saying that only a fool would search the labyrinth while Robert was still inside. He made comparisons with jumping off a cliff to see how high it was.

But love and loyalty are not easy to dismiss and when everything seems lost, what else is there to lose?

The girls were resolute; they said they must go.

Lucien sighed, and shrugged.

'Well then, two final points – then I will have told you all that I have suspected or know. One is that Robert is very unstable. Franklin is growing old and everyone's aware that I shall not take his place. Which leaves Robert vulnerable, and terrified that without outside help all his dreams will be lost.

'Which makes him impatient and reckless, so much so that even my grandfather and Martha are wary now. They have been nervous for some time, which is why they fastened bolts across the cellar's exit points.'

Lucien went on, 'Secondly, although Robert is strong he's not immortal yet, and thus could be destroyed. If the right moment arose he could be consigned into that empty realm he tries so hard to avoid.'

'Do you mean we could kill him – if we had to?' Amy said.

Lucien said, 'Possibly. I cannot tell you how, though; after five hundred years my ancestor is skilled at preserving his own life. But there is an old and rare book in which this has been discussed – such things often intrude on superstitious lore. The modern world knows much, yet often overlooks pathways it once explored.'

'Is there a copy of the book inside the house?'

'My grandfather has one which he's used for research. He says it's 'dangerous'. He keeps it in a chest in the library study.'

The book had to be seen.

Lucien escorted the girls along a circuitous route, to avoid discovery.

While they crept into the silent library he remained outside in the hall. He was to stand as their lookout against Franklin and Martha. He was as nervous as a kitten, and the girls prayed that his nerve would not desert him now. But they had no time to comfort him, for they had work to do. They had to grope their way across the unlit room. They had to find the study door, open it without a sound and sneak inside ...

Once within, they lit the paraffin lamp and raised the worn wick just enough to drive the worst shadows back.

They quickly searched the room and found a chest beneath the desk. Lugged it to centre stage, then found it locked courtesy of Chubb. Amy wielded a letter knife in an attempt to release the catch but the blade of the knife snapped halfway up.

Growing more frustrated and conscious of fleeting time Caroline used a brass candlestick to bypass the obdurate lock. She smashed it several times, having first wrapped the 'club' in a length of musty cloth.

The chest at last yielded, and Amy moved the lamp closer.

They peered within.

Assorted items: jewellery, books and diaries. Black and white photographs of Franklin as a child; some of a young Martha when she was no more than nine or ten. Fair hair in long pigtails, smiling, stunningly thin – no hint of the whale to come. Martha had been photographed at the rear of Gehenna's yard. The place was lusher then: flower-beds covered the ground. The glare of summer sun was shining in Martha's eyes. And she looked innocent.

But a figure with her – her mother possibly – a tall, imposing form, sternly ignoring her, suggested bleaker things: menace and misery, black secrets in her soul. For though it was no more than thirty-five years old, the woman's face was cold and its look bitter and drawn. Her eyes were so sunken they were like bullet holes, while her mouth was thin, tight and pursed. And even at that stage of Martha's fateful life the message was quite clear: her future was doomed. Her mother had succumbed to the grim enchantments of the dark brooding house on the moor ...

'Which book do you think it is?'

'Let's take them all, Amy. We can read them when we're in Lucien's room ... '

The three retraced their steps, careful not to attract Franklin's attention. Once ensconced in Lucien's room they spread their pillage out. A stack of leather-bound books – much handled, often read. One in particular attracted Amy's eye, being more dog-eared than the rest. It appeared that Franklin, ever anxious to preserve his longed-for destiny, had scoured this book the most. Seeking to be forewarned, lest retribution come. Planning to be forearmed ... *The Science of Necrophobes*, by Professor Jonathan Mort-Coves. *A Propositional Work*.

A daunting title, and an even more daunting book. Densely printed pages, diagrams and family maps. The kind of turgid work that winds up at the back of library storerooms.

But it was not distraction that the girls were looking for. They were looking for concrete help for their dealings with Robert.

Preferably a detailed plan for consigning him to Hell.

Or wherever he belonged ...

Page 1: " ... that which we may thus term a 'necrophobe' will be possessed of the rare facility to perpetuate by some means its own morbid existence. Unlike, for example, zombies – the dead returned to life – a necrophobe survives by somehow evading death: in the same way that 'truth' exists only through the act of being observed, 'Death' must be a witness. If we take 'existence' to be – "

'Are you getting any of this?'

Caroline gave a frown. 'I got the first two lines. He lost me after that.'

'Me too,' Amy muttered. 'Move on a few pages.'

On page 3: "The elemental force cannot be shaped or bound - nor fashioned in this state. It can be altered – ie transmogrified: its constituent parts limitlessly rearranged. Thus, ice appears as snow, or water, or as mist – or as nothing at all. If mist is so dispersed that it cannot be recognized, at what point does it cease to be water at all? Does it merge into air? Is it, in fact, the air? Or something in between?"

'Skip on – '

Page 17: "The fundamental state of death may defy

definition. Is a 'dead' log dead if it contains living cells? Is an electron 'dead' if its orbit decays?''

'Good grief!'

Page 49: ''Concession to a fact quite simply makes that fact actually come to be. In non-existence, refusal to exist is as pertinent a force as a being's desire to live: the mere acknowledgement of either, and/or both cannot simply be dismissed. Thus, when a sceptic pleads that it is impossible to penetrate the veil of universal cause, the shade of his belief must be that for good or ill nothing cannot be proven. Which leads directly to the question of the role of existence itself – beyond that which is known in corporeal terms. If man, for all his works – ''

Caroline slammed shut the book. Before it numbed her brain. Amore measured second look offered the girls a fraction more: but not so much that they felt cheered.

The crucial comment: ''It has thus been proposed that the very fabric of the necrophobic form employs a contra-force to hold itself intact - what might be called one negative aspect of the ancients' assessment of the universal form. Thus, if the positive aspects can in some manner be attuned to a concerted assault on this antithetic void – earth, water, air and fire – it may affect the very basis of this coil we stand upon! To harmonize these four – to wield the four as one: to turn nature itself into an avenging tool: this very well may be the conundrum's resolve – and may produce results … ''

Amy put the dog-eared book down. 'The 'ancient elements'. Where do we get them from?'
'They are all around us,' Caroline said, confused. 'The natural forces of nature – everywhere.'
'But how do we *use* them? How can we fight with air? What weapon is the 'earth'?'

'Do you know, Lucien?' Caroline said, turning towards him.

Lucien shook his head. 'This is all beyond me. Perhaps if he appears you'll recognize a clue – '

'And if not?'

'You will die.'

47

Hardly armed to the teeth, but intent on seeing this business through, the girls abandoned further thought.

They had exchanged ideas, suggestions and theories, but had moved no closer to solving the professor's clue. Their only slender hope was that – as Lucien said – a resolution might appear.

Which was meagre comfort, but then they did not know if a 'weapon' could be forged or handled anyhow.

And Professor Mort-Coves' book might well have been the work of a scatterbrained old man.

Too in awe of Robert Jilkes to confront the labyrinth, Lucien declined to assist with their venture. He offered to remain close by the cellar door, and stand a patient guard. He would keep Franklin away, if he could control his spasmodically jerking limbs. He had pressed himself to the stage where both his strength and sanity teetered on a dangerous brink.

He was straining desperately to hold on to his thoughts as the girls slipped past the door and progressed into the gloom.

Sometimes his mind wandered so far into a void that he feared it might not return ...

As the heavy door swung shut, fear descended on the girls. For a time they had been too distracted to pay much attention to their doubts but they compensated for that now with a suffocating dread. They believed that *nobody* had ever been as exposed as they felt at that point.

They felt like two kittens tossed into a wolf cave.

But the girls possessed the sense to take Daniel's dog with them, and the dog seemed more at ease. She was not exactly serene, but nor would she permit that labyrinth to believe that it held the upper hand. All those patient canine years of straining to be top dog now stood Jess in good stead.

In order to demonstrate this, the dog tried a warning growl. The hackles on her back reared up – bristled – relaxed.

Though it was no picnic in there, the staunch lurcher believed that she could take on anything ...

48

As the tense group slowly advanced, the silence of the shafts descended on them like a shroud.

For yet one more time Gehenna's atmosphere tried to make the anxious girls believe they were in a tomb. It assaulted them with another of its gauntlets of warning, daring them to proceed. And in the lengthy canyons of obscurity between the lamps, the labyrinth teased the girls with the strongest of its trumps: providing them with a glimpse of the total blindness it could wield, if it felt so inclined …

An hour passed: nothing yet to overload the cart of stress which the girls hauled in their wake. So far they had witnessed little to make them more afraid than they had been at the start: they had heard no troubling sounds. So far their hearts still pumped, their senses were still keen, their responses were alert.

Indeed, so accustomed were they to a state of near-constant threat that a more passive condition would have appeared distinctly odd. Peace was a distant land which they had now left far behind. They had almost forgotten their pasts …

'The shotgun!' Caroline breathed, when she saw the cobalt gleam of gunmetal ahead. 'This is where I left Daniel!'

There was no trace of him now. He must have been carried off, the abandoned weapon the only remaining sign. Caroline increased her pace, stooped to pick up the gun, checked it –

'One cartridge left. I'm not sure that I would be willing to use it, though. Have you ever handled a gun?'

'Not yet.' Amy shook her head. 'But I'm prepared to learn.'

She took hold of the polished stock, felt the shotgun's weight pull against her arm. It was more alarming than she expected.

They stole cautiously on, in the manner of hesitant storks testing out a murky pond.

They crept past all the chambers, altars and cutting-slabs. Past all the ropes and chains, sledgehammers, stakes and knives. Past the remains of feasts – the gristle and tough skin which Robert tossed aside. The girls tried not to gag at this, tried their best not to inhale the rich, sickening stench which lingered in the air. Tried to avoid the flesh and bones which rotted beneath their feet. Tried to keep their mouths closed.

'Where's the dog going, Amy?'

Amy spun on her heels. Jess was loping away.

She said, 'Oh brilliant! She's going back to the house!'

'No, I don't think she is, I think she's caught a scent.'

'With all this meat around that's hardly surprising – this must be dog heaven.'

Caroline said, 'We should go after her in case she finds something!'

'If she starts *eating* it, count on me to throw up.'

The girls hurried behind as the grey dog's stride lengthened, and she whimpered anxiously.

After a time the lurcher stopped inside a nondescript and neglected side tunnel. There were no guttering oil lamps, nor any signs of rooms. The girls saw only grey sullen walls and an arched ceiling dripping gloom. Granite slabs on the floor had been polished apple-skin smooth by centuries of wear.

'There's nothing in here,' said Amy. 'Jess was wrong.'

She leaned back against a wall, needing to catch her breath.

As she did so a hidden door, disguised by stone cladding, swung silently ajar.

The girls warily probed into a small chamber which led to a flight of steps. The flight curved clockwise around a granite core, descending like the step in a castle's central tower. Tar brands carried surly flames whose light lay on the walls like raw, festering sores.

They began a long descent, as happy as skylarks trapped on a firing range. Even the powerful lurcher was beginning to hang back; the dog knew evil's smell, and it was thick in the air. Dogs, too, are prone to doubts and even canine hearts can be pushed too far.

Such claustrophobia was pressing on them all.

Such a sinister silence spiralled up from below.

Every step taken was a triumph of their courage over their urge to hightail it away.

At length, the group arrived at the innermost sanctum of Robert's bleak domain. The cold steps deposited them amongst a maze of shafts which had known so much death that its memory stained the stones. Stained them with tears and blood. With terrifying drawings of torment and despair.

The awful images were made more vibrant by the glow from massive iron braziers, throbbing with blood-red coals.

The light made the tunnels appear to pulse like the ventricles of a heart sealed in a granite chest.

Reluctantly the girls forsook the familiarity of the stairs – their only escape route.

They began advancing upon a nearby doorway, dreading what they would find and almost too scared to look.

They peeped cautiously in, then drew in enormous breaths when the room produced no threat.

In fact the chamber contained little of interest. Blankets and discarded clothes, souvenirs gathered over the years.

A broken charm bracelet. Next to it an engagement ring.

Overall, a strange sadness …

They ventured a few more steps towards a second door, as uninviting as the first.

They peered tentatively inside and clamped their hands to their mouths. The urge to scream was strong but they dared not make a sound. Before them, on a slab, clothed in an orange gown, was Daniel – bleeding and bound.

He had been savagely beaten: weals covered his face and his hands. But he was still conscious, and his eyes still held life's fire.

He was straining to escape, wanting to claim revenge for the torments he'd endured.

Soft as a kiss on silk, Caroline crept into the room to release and rescue her lover.

'We've come to get you out of here,' she whispered in his ear.

Daniel began to writhe. 'No – save yourselves!' he urged. 'The killer's still around, and he can move so fast – you mustn't take the risk. That's how he was able to capture me, he appears at such a pace. And this place is deceptive, the acoustics are all wrong. I'd no time to readjust once my first effort missed. You must leave this place now!'

But Caroline would not abandon him, and began to explore the room. She found a thin dagger on a square of red velvet.

She used it on the stubborn ropes, while Amy stood on guard, imploring her to be quick …

In a matter of moments they were fleeing the grim chamber, with Daniel leaning heavily on the shoulders of the girls.

He was in absolute agony – barely able to help himself. He had lost so much blood and such stiffness gripped his limbs. He hardly had the strength to pacify his dog, who was beside herself.

The lurcher was so elated at this apparent change in her canine luck that she kept tripping them up, and had to be subdued.

Amy suggested that they bind her mouth to stop her whimpering.

The girls' plan was to take Daniel out, then return like two church mice to search for Lou and Jade.

Their first real problem: getting back up the stairs. There was no room for three abreast so Daniel had to crawl. He had to drag his legs up the five hundred steps of the spiralling staircase.

Which took them – five years? A decade? Half a life? The interlude between the Big Bang and the termination of all time?

That's how long it seemed to be as the three strained to escape before the monster came.

They kept glancing behind them, but could only see so far: the staircase's gradual curvature created a large blind spot.

Robert might be on their heels, and they would never know.

Or he might be waiting up ahead …

But they reached the upper level unscathed, though Daniel's stamina was spent.

There was no time to pause to rest, though; they had to quickly press ahead. The girls grabbed Daniel's arms, exhorted him to run. Daniel gritted his teeth and forced his protesting legs to stumble along the shaft.

They were weaving like drunkards, bouncing off all the walls. They kept glancing behind, scouring the path ahead. Conscious of the fact that each second was worth its weight in gold. If not worth more than gold …

But for how long could they run? How long is a piece of string? Would their flight never end?

How many chambers and niches must they pass – how many looming voids and blind alleys were left? How many more footsteps – how many more heartbeats – how many more snorted breaths?

And if luck is a fickle friend, does that mean it will change just at the very point when all seems not quite lost? Just as the spirits rise fractionally; just a touch. One too many requests for luck …

For suddenly he came, racing through the dim shafts like a crazed animal.

Throwing off cunning, Robert launched his assault. Homed right in on the group like a heat-seeking missile. His mind consumed by hate, his heart blackened by rage and his eyes like amber fire.

Crippled and grotesque, legs twisted by the years, so that they powered him on like a great spider's limbs. Arms stretching out like claws, and lips curling back from teeth which would have shamed a corpse.

'*Amy!*' screamed Caroline as her friend slid to a halt, spun around and lifted the gun. 'He's moving too fast!'

'You go on!' Amy cried. 'I'll get him! I'm all right – I can handle this stuff!'

She struggled with the gun. How did she make it work? Was there a safety catch?

'I think I've got it! Just go – get Daniel out!'

She grimaced down the shaft – faltered – Caroline was right! The distance in between – *what distance?* – shrank as Robert ate it up.

'I'm going to get him!' she yelled, gripping the gun on a level with her waist and resting it against her hip.

'Trust me! Go, Caroline – run like you've never run! Run like the wind itself!'

49

Robert advanced on her. Forty-five metres off. Forty. No turning back.

Now down to thirty – twenty-five – *fire the gun!* What do you want, Amy? An invitation? Fire it now!

Twenty – time's running out – look deep into his eyes – *see that?* – that's death in there!

Now down to fifteen!

Amy shook like a leaf. The trigger felt so slender. What if it got jammed?

Twelve –

Had to fire it now. Had to –

Ten –

Fire it now. Had to –

She fired the gun …

* * *

The recoil of the weapon sent Amy staggering back and dumped her onto the floor. Virtually concussed by the shattering report she was nonetheless aware that she had caused Robert no harm. Her shot had hit the roof; the lead had been nullified, or deflected down the shaft. Which meant that in moments …

How long – could she work it out? Ten metres away at first and then she'd been flung back. The distance she had gained when the recoil threw her – another eight metres?

Whichever way Amy looked at it she ought to be dead by now; a turtle could have struck in less time than she took to count.

What had kept her alive?

She squinted down the shaft to see the reason why.

Robert had been almost blinded by stones blasted from the roof. Nothing life-threatening, but enough to slow him down.

Slow him sufficiently that Amy just had time to clamber to her feet.

All too soon that moment passed, and the blood from Robert's eyes trickled away like tears.

His anger solidified into a deep resolve: Amy would have to pay. For every shard of stone – for every blood-rich tear – she would pay a thousand times.

Amy could sense this, sense it as clear as day. Could sense it in every sound and gesture Robert made.

Sense it twitching in his hands. Sense it glistening on his teeth. Sense it glittering in his eyes.

She began to back away, stumbling and fumbling with the now useless gun.

She threw a glance behind her – her friends were still running. Perhaps they'd reach the house, perhaps she'd bought them time –

Time was all she had left – the greatest gift of all. Scarcely thought about until it ends.

And it was ending, was running out so fast. There was barely a pause long enough in which to draw a breath. For here he came again – ready to add one more name to his list of victims.

But all was not yet lost, for the lurcher – quiet so far – made an unexpected move. In the very instant that Robert moved to strike, Jess came in from his left in a tornado of snarls. She clamped her powerful jaws around Robert's left thigh and sank her fangs through his flesh. Robert started howling, and lashed out ferociously. A solid blow struck the dog, sent her careering back. But she rose quick as a flash to engage in a fresh attack, spurred on by her success.

For Jess knew she had hurt him – she had heard his gasp of pain. His blood was in her mouth and she'd torn strips from his leg. He would never race again – he would be forced to hobble now.

But Robert still posed a threat …

He quickly proved the fact by snatching up the dog – lifting her bodily.

He shook her viciously, as if he would loosen every joint and cartilage and make her bones fly apart. Flung her against a wall, then watched her land in a heap and heard her whimper with pain.

Then he chortled scornfully as the wounded dog crawled away. He hurled abuse after her as she sought a place to rest.

She had no more strength to fight. She had major injuries to her chest, and had given all she had.

As soon as Jess vanished Robert turned to resume his onslaught on Amy – even more bitter than before.

Dragging his torn leg, he strove to reduce the gap; for Amy had backed away during the dog's attack. She felt less disembodied now – her concussion had faded – she had the sense to retreat.

Amy took off, sprinting, hoping to rejoin her friends. If Daniel had spare cartridges they could reload the gun.

She was worried about Jess but, in the circumstances, could have done little to help ...

50

The three reached the cellar door at almost the same moment. Lucien had disappeared.

They felt too exposed there to risk reloading the gun. Who knew where Franklin lurked? Who knew when he might come? They thundered up the stairs towards the girls' bedroom. Then remembered it was locked.

If Lucien had been with them he might have shown them to one of his secret passages, but they were on their own. They would have to make a stand at the point where they were now, right there at the top of the stairs.

Which at least gave them the advantage of a commanding view. They could cover the hall and stairs, and the corridors above. It was just that – even in such straits – could they shoot somebody if the need should arise?

They would have to find that out if the need did arise. For now they just had to wait.

And it did not take long for sounds to come from below: the sounds of Robert Jilkes inside the labyrinth: now approaching the tunnel's end – trailing his injured leg – spitting curses and rage.

They could also hear Franklin, urging his master on. He was directly underneath, right by the cellar door.

No one had the slightest clue as to where Martha might be. They just hoped she would play no part.

But they made a grave error by neglecting Martha: the old woman was near. In fact she was so close they could have almost heard her breathe. She was a short distance along the hall, crouching in a dark doorway. Hunching like a bloated bug, her fingers curved like claws. Cunning thoughts in her mind …

And a few moments later she advanced – amazingly furtive for one of such massive bulk.

Martha was like an outlandish dancer as she snaked her way along the hall. Each foot was planted down with exaggerated care. She could have stepped on eggs and barely cracked the shells, so gently did she walk.

Indeed, so soft was her approach that she was almost on top of them before Amy glanced back and gazed straight into her eyes, where she could see nothing there but a glimmer of madness. A vivid and infernal fire …

Abandoning her stealth, Martha ran the last few steps like a charging bull. 'Look out!' cried Amy, as she raised her arms. 'She's trying to snatch the gun!' Daniel twisted to one side. But too late! He lost his grip on the polished walnut stock as Martha's hands swept down. 'Don't let her take it!' Amy made a frantic lunge.

Martha skipped back a step, clutching the captured gun. She giggled with delight and danced an ecstatic jig.

And that was her mistake.

For she was too close to the stairwell, too thrilled by her own success. Excitement dulled the edge of Martha's attentiveness.

As she danced back one more step, catastrophe occurred.

Martha began to fall …

The old woman's expression altered dramatically as her triumph was stripped away, and despair showed in its place.

Her pale eyes widened as the floor beneath her feet transformed into a well of malevolent intent. A place where gravity was irresistible, and balance redundant.

She gave a shrill scream, but it could not halt her fall. In fact, the sound appeared more like her own death knell.

As she tumbled down the stairs a veritable peal of screams was wrenched out of her slack throat.

A silence descended as Martha lay below, her neck grotesquely askew.

But the silence was short-lived, for Franklin was on his way. Franklin had heard the noise and guessed what it signified. By the time he reached the hall to confirm what he'd surmised, he was sobbing with grief.

'Oh, Martha – Martha!' he cried as he knelt down and cradled her in his arms with his brow pressed to her cheek. 'What have they done to you? Please don't abandon me, Martha – don't leave me now!'

And then Franklin looked up and saw three faces peering down. An overwhelming urge for vengeance rocked his mind.

He gently laid his sister's head on the cold hallway floor, then he advanced up the stairs.

51

'Leave them be,' a voice muttered, and Franklin promptly froze, as if he'd turned to stone.

Robert was emerging from his labyrinthine home – dragging his injured leg – his fury under control. Now that the three were trapped he was content to take his time, and enjoy the coming kill.

'I don't want them damaged. Their souls must be intact.'

'Yes, Master,' Franklin breathed. 'It's just – they've killed Martha.'

''Tis no matter,' Robert said. 'She was a bloated crone of no significance. And no use to us now.'

Robert stopped to look around the hall.

'Much has passed since I was last here. Yet it looks much the same as in Lord Cornwell's time. That old fool! Had me banned – yet here I am alive, while he fed coffin worms.'

He stepped over Martha and paused at the foot of the stairs. His scornful, callous gaze locked for an instant on the girls.

Then he began to climb, leaving a trail of blood like paint stains on the stairs.

He had scarcely begun his ascent when a distraction emerged from the shadows in the hall. It was the earnest Lucien, straining to stay composed while each nerve he possessed felt ready to explode. He was trying to calm his limbs, trying to prevent his heart from failing in his chest.

Yet it was not Robert who seemed the most surprised, rather it was a shocked Daniel who came out with a gasp. He sensed this was the man he'd fought with in the barn, several fraught hours before.

He whipped his fists up, ready to fight again. But relaxed when it became clear that the focus was not on him. For it was the necrophobe who filled Lucien's thoughts and held all his attention.

'Master – ' Lucien said. 'You shall not take their souls, you have caused harm enough. It is now your time to die!'

Robert ignored the words, and continued his ascent.

Lucien picked up the fallen shotgun, dwarfing it with his hands, and aimed it at Robert's back.

He cried, 'One more step and I shall shoot without remorse!'

'As you please,' Robert said, seemingly unperturbed.

He had long ago dismissed his sickly descendant as being of little worth.

The shotgun's firing pin hammered against an expended cartridge case.

Lucien threw the gun down, and began to mount the stairs.

'Master!'

Robert Jilkes sighed, bored rather than concerned.

'Leave me – '

Lucien closed in. His hands bunched into fists. He summoned all his strength.

'I have to end this, for it has gone too far! My life has been a waste but I can give it worth.'

'Ignore him!' Franklin cried. 'Go on to take the girls!'

'I *am* trying,' Robert sighed.

Lucien gathered himself, drew in all of his power and all the resentment that he bore. He knew this was his moment – his chance to assuage the guilt heaped on him by his kin through their hideous lives. His donation to the world, before his own sad world faded to full darkness.

Which it was doing more rapidly each day.

His Huntington's chorea was a relentless force.

'I'm dying,' he muttered.

Robert was unimpressed.

'People die all the time … '

Still Robert ascended, hauling his injured leg as though it was attached to a huge iron ball and chain. He was on the point of victory; he knew that for a fact. The girls could not escape – their souls would soon be his. And yet he felt a pang of sadness in his heart, a yearning for Agnes.

For what if he could not save her, could not return her from the grave? What if her body was so crushed and empty that she was lost? *People die all the time.* And on those who are left behind rests the burden of despair …

'*Master!*'

Again the voice.

Robert Jilkes turned around, seeking to dredge up an insult.

He was still thinking when Lucien raised his arm and plunged a gleaming knife hilt-deep into Robert's chest. The unexpected blow was aimed straight at the heart, and the necrophobe swayed back.

Lucien moved with him, threw his weight against the knife and employed his fearsome strength to drive the cruel point home. His eyes became seething pools of energy – so great was his effort, so deadly his intent.

Yet his face blanched suddenly, and he stumbled backwards a pace –

Doubt flooded through his mind, made every fibre quake –

For Robert seemed unharmed and, with his clawlike hands, he pulled the long blade out.

'Foolish child,' Robert said, and an ominous dispassion was evident in his tone. 'You mean nothing to me – have you not yet surmised that much? Loyalty to blood and kin have no place in my heart. I would as soon kill you as kill a cockroach!'

Lucien hit him hard. Though he had been weakened by his damaging lifestyle he called on years of hate to add venom to his fist. He aimed a thunderous blow right at the centre of Robert's impassive face.

It should have stunned him – should have sent him sprawling back. But Robert barely flinched, just gave the slightest smile.

Then he said, 'Cease, Lucien. No more vexation; no more gnat-like attacks. No more – '

He gave a grunt as he was punched again.

'No more – '

Again a punch.

'No – '

Yet another punch.

Robert's detachment snapped.

As if enveloped by the rage of a forest fire, Robert's volatile blood seethed and fury filled his brain. Prudence died in the flames – sanity was dispersed by an incandescent flash.

All other concerns were brusquely swept aside as a primitive desire for violence took control. The sole thought in Robert's mind was that punishment was due to all who opposed him.

Lucien backed away, retreating along the hall as Robert's wrath approached.

The necrophobe's face was a leathery death mask. His scorpion-like limbs were flexing – set to strike. His hands were reaching out and his rotting nails were knives destined for Lucien's eyes.

Every last fibre of Robert seemed intent on claiming some portion of Lucien for itself. A severed tongue or ear, a lock of greying hair or an organ from his chest. Some small memento of the time when evil turned upon its own bloodline and slew one of its own kin. A prize to mark the fact that evil knows no bounds in its effort to exist …

Lucien could not confront such a terrifying display of naked malevolence. He judged discretion to be his only prudent course and turned on his startled heels. He pounded downstairs and fled the house. He hoped the threat would fade once he was out of sight, that Robert's anger would subside.

But his nightmare followed – for Robert forsook the house. For the first time in aeons he stepped into the world.

Leaving the three stunned friends, and Franklin following, striving to keep up, shouting, *'The sacrifice, Master! The sacrifice!'*

52

The three friends pursued them to the yard, hoping to find a way to assist Lucien. They were quite startled to discover that dawn had arrived. Tension had wiped out time and a whole night had expired. They hardly required the lamp that Caroline had grabbed, thinking it was still dark.

While they were in the cellar, a breeze had reached the moor. It had raised the temperature a fraction, stirred the fog. For the first time in days the land could take a breath, and shrug its mantle off.

At an ever-increasing tempo the fog was being dispersed. Its banks were rolling back, ragged and disarrayed. And with the change was born some hope: for it seemed as though the world was fighting back at last ...

But of more pressing concern was the scene which was revealed when the three gazed across the yard.

The enraged Robert was wading through the swamp, intent on bringing down the fleeing Lucien. Both had sunk past their knees – both of them were wallowing like creatures of the mud.

Franklin was some way behind them, rooted to drier ground. Pleading without success for his master to return.

Not for his grandson's sake but because the old man craved more soul-sacrifices.

Franklin's plea was futile, though; Robert would have none of it. He had fixed his sights on his treacherous, frightened kin. The sacrifice could wait. The hunt for souls was now firmly relegated to second place.

As Lucien ploughed on, Robert panted behind – almost blinded by the morning sun. Robert had not seen daylight for nigh on five hundred years. His skin had not been touched by its damaging rays. He vowed – when this was done – he would never be provoked to leave his home again. How could they stand it, those mortals on the earth? How could they bear the pain that the cruel sunlight brought? They should retreat like him. Eke out their entire lives in some dark labyrinth ...

53

Lucien had to rest. He found it hard to breathe; his lungs seemed full of lead. The explanation: the air was full of gas. Methane had bubbled up from the dense mud of the swamp. It had been trapped by the fog but, as the fog lifted, so the methane escaped.

It still could not disperse, though, in its usual fashion, for it was meeting compression from the smoke-like haze above. All it could do was lurk, invisible and rank, like a bane upon the earth.

In fact, so much gas was released by decaying matter that its concentration had gone past the point at which it could be considered safe.

The whole surface of the swamp and the noxious layer above were like bombs seeking a fuse ...

Lucien tried to battle on but, desperate as he was, the mud's pull slowed him down. He lacked the hardened resilience and power of his demented ancestor, who had grappled with death and won. He lacked the force of will and the crazed, obsessive rage which Robert thrived on.

Only time shielded Lucien from his fate, the time that it would take for his strength to dissipate. For Robert would never stop. If it took a thousand years he would run Lucien down.

So then, what was the point of running? What value was there in trying to hide?

What was he gaining? What were mere seconds worth? Should he not end this now and accept his dreadful doom? Should he not –

Lucien froze as his gaze danced across the swamp, right back to Gehenna's yard. There he saw the two girls, and Daniel, watching him anxiously. He saw the brass lantern glinting at Caroline's side. He breathed the methane gas and knew that he had spied the means to thwart Robert at last.

He cupped his grey, calloused hands like a funnel around his mouth, drew in a massive breath and yelled for all he was worth.

'*Throw the lantern!*' he cried. '*For my sake – throw the lamp!*'

But no one seemed to hear.

Sensing final defeat, Lucien watched helplessly as Robert closed in on him. He felt virtually paralysed – like a man swathed in ropes. He felt like a non-swimmer who had strayed out of his depth. His only hope lay with three allies, and they'd failed to hear his cries.

He would have been so *willing* to die if only he could, right at the very end, claim some dignity back. This all seemed so futile, so pointless, such a waste: to die like a cornered rat.

In a surge of desperation he shouted once again. Emitted such a cry that his larynx almost snapped.

'*The lantern! Throw the lamp!*'

And this time he was heard. Caroline knew what he meant.

But she couldn't do it. 'It will kill Lucien, too,' she said.

Amy said, 'He knows that, Caroline.'

'OK – *you* do it.' Caroline gestured at the lamp. It was glimmering on the ground.

'You can't do it, either,' said Caroline. 'It's too much. Even to save our lives we can't just let Lucien die. We can't abandon him after he's tried so hard to give us all a chance.'

'What *can* we do, though? We can't destroy Robert. But if we simply wait he's certain to kill us!'

'We're left with Hobson's choice.'

'*Pass the lantern to me. I shall kill him –* ' breathed a voice.

* * *

The startled girls spun round.

A hideous figure had crawled out of the house. She was like a large doll formed from leather, pitch and oil. She pulled herself along on pitifully thin arms. Her voice was like a brittle leaf crushed in a human palm. Maggots dripped from her tongue.

And in the empty socket where her left eye should have been there was nothing but a void: a terrifying black hole.

And from her right eye there hung a tear, like a raindrop set to fall. And the raindrop was stained with blood.

The frightened girls backed off as the gruesome doll approached, gasping at every move.

She croaked: 'I am Agnes – the love of his life. A woman once fair, and pretty in my face. So pretty he once said I was the only light that could burn in his world.'

The woman folded herself around a rasping cough, paused for a moment, drained – then dragged her suffering on,

'But the light which touched his world has all but guttered out. And it is time for rest … '

54

For twenty-seven years Agnes had lain within a bitter, lonely tomb. She had heard voices at times and the scrape of spades. She had heard the old man search, though he never arrived; always he had turned away at the decisive moment to try his luck elsewhere. Perhaps if Franklin had discovered her during those early frightened years then nothing would have changed and Agnes would have continued as before. But hopelessness appeared and, through that hopelessness, Agnes sensed oblivion …

* * *

'I passed through times,' she breathed, 'when I came close to death, so wretched were my thoughts. I heard no voices – no digging – saw no lamps. I had no hope at all that I would be released. Forced to eat grubs and voles, their flesh so sinewy and spare it could scarce nourish me. And for company – which was what I craved the most – I conversed with the rocks, and sometimes they spoke back. The rocks said, 'Why go on? Come lie here with us until the end of time … '

'All those years,' Agnes said, 'with nothing but my dreams. And memories of love. We loved like children in those first, fearful days. Loved with all that we had – our love kept us alive. Loved with a passion such as none but desperate souls can even contemplate.

'And surely,' Agnes sighed, 'no one had ever been as desperate as we two?'

At an agonizing pace, Agnes advanced upon the flickering lantern.

She could see its thin flame like a halo in the yard – the final poor reward for the torments she endured: the pain in every limb, the scorching of each pore and the searing of her soul.

'But in the darkness where I thought I should die, I slept through such a peace as I have never known. A peace which swept me up and compelled me to weep with joy and gratitude. Rest is so precious – calmness brings such relief when one has spent so long struggling to exist. I thought, *If only he – my beloved Robert – could share this peace with me …*

'Why did we strain so hard to live inside the dark? How much did we neglect? All our ambitions were so warped by the years that sometimes we forgot the people we once had been. Dreams became abandoned, our hopes were overlooked; we forgot everything. Even our descendants were moulded into serfs: vassals to gather food, wardens trained to destroy. And it was not like that when our life first began. Why did we lose so much?'

Agnes was forced to rest, forced to grapple with pain for control of her limbs.

Like an injured spider she convulsed on the muddy ground; pink foam bubbled from her lips and her eye socket filled with dirt. So repugnant did she appear that no one moved to help, they were too horrified.

Indeed, to offer help would have been to squander breath, for nothing on this earth could have aided Agnes then. She had strayed too far beyond anything humankind could possibly supply.

'Something stirred,' Agnes gasped, when spasms eased their grip on her withered throat muscles. 'Something inside me responded to a cry rent from my lover's soul – a forlorn, anguished howl. A howl through which the grief which hides beneath his rage showed pitiful and clear. For Robert's lost now – cast adrift like a leaf on the indifferent stream which wends its way through time. He dreads that I will not return, no matter how he strives. He fears Agnes has died. And without me there, then all his hopes are crushed. He must wander alone – eternally unloved. Doomed to dwell in a world where nothing moves but ghosts and shadows wreathed in despair ...

'And could I be unmoved by my beloved's grief?' the brittle voice whispered. 'Could I forsake Robert in his most wretched state? Could I stand cruelly by while pains wrenched him apart? As weakened as I was – as hurtful as my wounds were – I knew he needed me. I summoned energy I thought had long expired. I gathered up a strength which I thought had long been lost. And now I have returned to guide him towards peace. And to lay his soul to rest ...'

55

An age seemed to have passed since Agnes first appeared, though nothing much had changed. Robert was still advancing on the petrified Lucien; Franklin was still screeching, trying to call him back. Not one of them observed the gruesome, twisted shape which was inching their way.

Agnes had the squat brass lantern in one withered hand and was sliding it ahead as she advanced on the swamp. Was creeping like a scorched insect through a string of shallow pools left behind by the fog.

A fearsome spectacle of chaos and carnage unfurled before the girls. They saw the irate figure of Franklin glance cursorily behind, then freeze when he saw the small, monstrous figure which approached. Watched as his startled eyes bloomed like pale summer flowers and heard his attempt to speak.

But the old man's throat locked, and the only sound produced was a high-pitched strangled squeak with no strength to endure. As fast as it appeared, it vanished – as did all the blood in his cheeks.

He staggered backwards, almost to the edge of the swamp. At that point he changed his mind and lurched drunkenly ahead. He tried to approach Agnes, thought better of it and faltered, caught between stools.

Shock and bewilderment took command of his face. He tried once more to speak; once more nothing emerged. If he guessed Agnes's intention, he was too befuddled to turn thoughts into sense.

Agnes squirmed stoically on; Franklin did not receive even so much as the briefest of glances. All of her attention was now directed on the swamp, the gas of which had formed a thin haze in the air. She had crawled desperately close to the point of no return, and oblivion lay near.

Which was her aim, of course – the sanctuary of peace. The resting place for those with no strength left to toil.

Alas, she had not allowed for her lover's anguished gaze to fall upon her face.

Through the faint haze of methane, through the shimmering of his tears, Agnes still looked beautiful.

Robert had never once wavered in his devotion to his love; had never once believed there could be a woman more fair. Agnes was his sole desire – the purpose of his life – the keeper of his heart. And when his fraught gaze fell on her his face lit up with joy. The weight of centuries slipped aside, and he felt handsome and young.

Forsaking Lucien, who was beyond further action, he strove to reach her arms …

Agnes slumped, statue-still – the only sign of life a faint trembling in her hands.

Inside, though, she was writhing; her heart felt torn apart. She suffered agonies through just seeing Robert's smile.

Would her torment never end?

Could life not simply cease?

Must she ache through all of time?

56

Agnes could bear no more. Summoning all her strength, she let the lantern fly.

It hurtled skywards, pierced the first layer of mist.

Soared like a brilliant bird with feathers of glass and gold.

Paused at its highest point.

Hung for a million years.

'*Forgive me*,' Agnes breathed …

The lamp began to fall, like a dying comet with a potent seed on board.

It reached the mist layer and shot through it like a bullet. Burst into clearer air, then fixed its sights on the earth. Approached the band of gas and swooped like a hungry hawk.

Whumph! Armageddon roared.

For a startled moment raging flames cloaked the mud. Yellow and pale blue spears tried to engulf the world. Air crackled in a heat so fierce that hair and clothing charred, and water turned to steam.

In the selfsame instant, a shock wave hit the yard with such ferocity that the three friends' innards jumped. It tore breath from their lungs, stripped moisture from their eyes and caused exposed skin to scorch.

They were all thrust backwards by the pressure of the wave and threw up their hands and arms to shield themselves from the fire, which sucked every scrap of methane from the swamp, and darkened half the sky…

But such drama was reduced to insignificance by the fate which befell the rest. To those unfortunate souls who were caught inside the blast, a mere scorching of skin would have seemed mild fare indeed. Agnes was turned to ash. Lucien was burned alive. Franklin's skin puckered and writhed.

It seemed to them that only Robert had been able to resist the urgent pleas of death and to stubbornly exist.

Such existence as it was, for the necrophobe's life-force had been dramatically reduced.

Yet, incredibly, he advanced – though dense flames curled all around, and his lungs were breathing smoke. It was sheer strength of will which propelled him through the mire: five centuries of pain, five centuries of lust, five centuries in which torment had steeled itself to confront such an hour.

And from all those years of scheming and the pains that he'd endured, he drew the strength to roar. It shook Gehenna's walls: *'Vengeance will now be mine! Eternity draws near! Evil demands your souls!'*

The flames at Robert's back danced like ecstatic snakes as he clambered from the swamp.

He brought fire with him, for it had fastened to his clothes. It was feasting on his skin like ravenous wolves. It lapped at his teeth and hair, his tongue, his fingernails: everything it could reach.

It was ferocious, yet could not make him stop. It could not make him yield, show mercy or forget.

He swore he'd never die. Swore he'd take mortal souls, consume them and survive ...

The group tried to back away, tried to flee to the house, but their limbs would not respond.

Daniel and the girls seemed riveted to the ground on which they stood. Their minds were blocks of stone – no thinking could intrude. The three were so afraid that everything seized up, and all strength and reason stalled.

Which left them dithering like sacrificial lambs as Robert Jilkes advanced – stumbling, dripping fire.

They would almost certainly have died if Franklin had not intervened. He saved them by default ...

The old man was gripped by rage, and all his venom was aimed straight at his ancestor.

Franklin felt cheated: he had laboured all his life in the belief that, come his time, he would receive his due tribute. But he now saw that entry to the mysterious realm of necrophobes would be denied him.

Franklin saw that his master despised him – was selfish, vicious and cruel. Robert would never divulge the secrets of his world. The secrets which were the only goal, ambition and desire of the angry Franklin. Now there would be no glorious merging with the dark forces of the earth. No empire would be spawned; no dynasty formed. At the end he would die – just as his own parents had died. Alone, unrewarded and unmourned.

So then, what had it all been for – the toil and sacrifice, the servitude and worship? Franklin's god had failed him; his god possessed feet of clay. Franklin's god was a noisome plague unfit to walk the earth. Whatever secrets lurked would always be concealed by misery and pain.

Robert could not share them for they were not his to share: his secrets were the curse of some dark, aberrant force.

At the end the truth had dawned that Robert was a false idol, and Franklin's faith had been betrayed.

The old man flung himself across the few metres of earth which separated them. He was like an enraged animal as he fell on Robert's back; his scorched fingers were claws closing around Robert's neck. His eyes were black with spite and his teeth were jagged knives. His lips slavered with bile.

Decades of envy and resentment fuelled the urge to grind the necrophobe's old bones and tendons into mush. Franklin felt sinews snap like string and saw a gleam of fear emerge in Robert's eyes.

But several centuries of existence do not come to an end simply to please an old man's wish. After some moments of confusion Robert Jilkes responded. His surprise disappeared and his ancient wrath returned. He gathered up his strength, felt fury fill his veins, and he began to battle back.

His corded muscles collided with the force of Franklin's insane rage: a mighty boulder hitting a massive rock.

Like two demented wolves they scuffled and they snarled, right to the swamp's charred edge …

57

Against a lurid backcloth of swirling flames and mud the combatants neared their end. All of their attention was devoted to the fight and they had little left to spare to wonder what might happen. Even if they had known, it is probable that they were too far gone to stop.

For some things are destined, and beyond mortal control. Some things wait centuries for their time to come. Such things cannot be turned off once all their elements have been put into place.

And so it was on this day, when a puzzle was resolved, when an old man's arcane theory was tested and approved. When Professor Mort-Coves' 'four' – *earth, water, air and fire* – combined to destroy a beast.

Nature itself, it seems, has ways of dealing with life's aberrations. Against the darkness, nature can proffer light. To thwart unending life she wields the noose of time. Corrupting lies are doomed when nature summons up a fierce, terrible truth.

For there is no creature on earth, nor in realms below, which can for ever foil the destiny of death.

And those who oppose nature will one day have to pay – for nature's memory is long.

Franklin and Robert Jilkes tumbled into the swamp, battling for their lives.

Mud roiled around them and flames danced, crackled and writhed. Ferociously hot air scorched their lungs and seared their eyes. Steam burst from ruptured cells to form horrific sores and blisters on their hands.

But fury gripped them and madness controlled their minds. They had grown oblivious to pain, their thoughts were blind. The only aim each of them had was to destroy the one who threatened to kill him.

Panting and snarling, grappling and punching. Pummelling with their heads, their hands, their knees, their feet. Straining to find the one decisive blow or kick which would win the day. They wrestled this way and that, forwards and back. Floundering in the mud – panicking – clawing their way out. Bloodstained and spitting curses. Their lips puffy and raw. Fighting until the end.

And it proved to be Robert who had the stronger grip and the greater endurance.

He locked his left arm around Franklin's scrawny neck. Braced it with his right hand – tightened it – forced him back. Inexorably bore down until Franklin's anxious face was buried in the ooze.

And then he held him, brought all his weight to bear. Pinned the thrashing old man while swamp mud filled his lungs.

And Franklin's struggles grew increasingly feeble – until at last they ceased.

But in Robert's mutant blood, evil and viciousness were coming under threat.

Dark seeds within him sensed an approaching force. The primal essences of life were being deployed. Darkness could feel the fire which raged into the air. It could feel, too, the clinging mud.

The mud was water and earth – the final links in the chemical chain which would undo the beast.

The four elements coalesced and released their ancient power to purify Robert.

58

The necrophobe grunted while Franklin's dead body rolled sluggishly in the mud. He felt victorious and turned to snarl his pride. Turned to inform the world that he had conquered time. He believed he would never die – thought he had braved the realm of sunlight and survived.

Nothing could prevent him from striding on the earth, from extending his dominion and confirming his reign.

Only his own free will – only if he should choose.

But then retribution came …

* **

Like a devastating horde of voracious parasites, Death's agents went to work. Robert Jilkes staggered as bolts of cleansing light lanced their way through his skin – scoured a route through his flesh. Seeking his evil source, they devoured all they touched and invaded every pore.

Great waves of conflict ran through his stunned muscles. His tortured frame writhed and his eyes began to bulge. The necrophobe's body became a battleground for opposing forces as light and darkness struggled to occupy the same physical space, the same moment in time.

The membranes of Robert's cells parted as evil quailed, and sought to escape. It departed in stages. First, through a sheen of blood. Then through more persistent spurts; then an orgiastic flood. Until all that could be seen was a gruesome red fountain of disintegrating flesh.

* * *

From the glistening remains of Robert's shattered chest there crept an eerie form. Born of the darkness, it hissed on seeing daylight. Like a vulture it crouched on the steaming corpse for a moment. Visible at its core was the throbbing, evil heart of nothingness itself.

Then the creature soared up, huge wings pounding the air. Its outline blurred the sky and shadows fell across the earth -

But it was rapidly dispersed, torn apart by the gusting wind.

And the curse of Robert Jilkes was scattered far and wide.

59

What little then remained of the fallen necrophobe was engulfed by the hungry swamp.

All that was left was a span of silence, a silence so profound that it seemed to be of a time when the planet was newly born. A time when all was peace. When evil had not learned to stride upon the world.

It was a silence which numbed the three who had survived: the two girls and Daniel, battered but still alive.

Faced with one final task.

The probing of Gehenna's depths.

Seeking their missing friends.

THE END

Peter Beere is the bestselling author of YA and adult thrillers, mysteries, fantasies, horror novels and social drama.

He lives in Somerset UK with his wife and dog.